The
Cloud
of
Deception

The
Cloud
of
Deception

Tracy Anne Bertini

Library of Congress Control Number: 2017911906
ISBN: Hardcover   978-1-5434-4089-8
                   Softcover   978-1-5434-4090-4
                   eBook   978-1-5434-4091-1

Print information available on the last page.

Rev. date: 07/31/2017

To order additional copies of this book, contact:
Xlibris
1-888-795-4274
www.Xlibris.com
Orders@Xlibris.com
764401

To my family, both new and old. You are each an inspiration and continually push me to reach for the stars. I am humbled and blessed to have such wonderful people with me on this journey we call life. I love you all.

To my husband and best friend, you will forever be my always. Thank you for allowing me to be me. I love you with all my heart.

PROLOGUE

"IN WORLD NEWS tonight, travel overseas has now been suspended to try to slow a deadly virus down. CDC spokesperson Ms. Hardy has been quoted as saying, 'This could be the virus that wipes out a large number of the human population.' The CDC and the World Health Organization have compiled a board of top scientists and physicians from many countries across the globe. The Denver International Airport and Hartsfield Jackson Airport have now suspended services." The newscaster continued with the story on the radio as Anya drove down Dahlonega Highway toward Cumming when, all of a sudden, everything went black.

"Wait, where am I?" Everything around her was still, as if a thick, soft gray fog were engulfing her and her surroundings. Looking around, she could see and hear nothing. *Where am I?* she thought. The silence was almost deafening. She was alone.

After a few moments of silence, she found herself in a conversation but could not hear the one initiating it. It was as if they were communicating telepathically. In true Anya style, she demanded to know what was going on. *Where am I, and who the heck is behind all of this!* She would pause in her rant as if listening to the voice in her head. *But I don't understand. I am not done yet! I have so much to do. What about . . .* She was silent; once again, the voice communicated with her. *No, this can't be how it ends. I'm not ready. Please give me more time. This can't be it*, she pleaded.

The voice was calm, reassuring, and unwavering; it gave her a sense of peace. The calmness and peace washed over her very soul. She continued to question what had happened and how this could truly be the end. She finally took a deep breath as she realized this really was how it was going to end.

CHAPTER ONE

A S SHE SAT at the weathered kitchen table, slowly drinking her morning brew, Anya watched the sunrise over the mountains. Quietly, in the background, she could hear the trickling of the stream that ran behind the old cabin. These mornings always brought back so many warm memories of her childhood and visiting this very cabin with her grandmother. The cabin was and always would be her happy place.

For the last four years since her grandmother's passing, Anya has restored the cabin to its former rustic beauty, from the gorgeous knotted hardwoods to the large hanging antique barn doors. Each project was completed with thought and care. The distraction of the remodel has helped numb her from the pain of losing her favorite person.

Sonya, her grandmother, had taught her many things over the years, from cooking to style pointers and, of course, how to be a lady. Growing up in Germany during World War II, Sonya had many stories to share but kept them to herself, or so it seemed. She always taught Anya to be strong, independent, and honest, which wasn't hard as Anya was always known for her stubborn and headstrong personality. It seemed the apple didn't fall from the tree.

Sipping her coffee, she remembered many games of hide-and-seek, cooking lessons, and of course the best bedtime stories. All her grandmother's bedtime stories had adventure and suspense but always ended the same way with a lesson to be learned. Anya could recite them by heart after years of hearing the same stories over and over.

As the sun rose, she could see the dew glistening on the flowers just outside on the porch. This was one of her favorite times of the day; the outside world was quiet and still. Anya slowly opened the French doors that led to the porch, letting in the crisp, fresh mountain air. She stepped outside into this new day feeling happy and nostalgic, having no idea what chain of events has already started miles away and how it would turn her life upside down in only a few hours.

Anya always started her day this way and eased into the morning routine of watering her flowers while finishing her coffee. She was a creature of habit—the same routine day in and day out—and she found it comforting to stay in her little box. Midmorning was always yoga time; over the last few years, Anya took pride in her somewhat mediocre yoga skills. She stepped back into the kitchen to get her yoga mat from the small closet in the narrow hall near the front door. Every morning, the sun shone through the stained-glass window that sat over the landing on the wooden staircase, making a beautiful-colored design on the hall floor. She stepped into the colored sunlight and could feel the warmth beneath her feet; as she stood, she took a deep breath and thought, *Life is good.*

Meanwhile, miles away, a meeting was just getting under way as everyone scurried around the conference table in the executive board room; one chair still was empty. "What was the holdup? Where could he be? The meeting is every Monday at 8:00 a.m. sharp with no exception. Every damn Monday, same time, same place for the last ten years with little to no change, no progress." Each department was with their status report and predictions of how the new tests would be tweaked and carried out for the following week. "He never runs late. Stacy, did you call his cell? Has anyone e-mailed or texted to find out where the hell he is!"

Stacy moved into the office next door and frantically dialed the phone for what seemed like the hundredth time, only to be met with no answer once again. *What should I do?* She sat and pondered. *Who should I call?* Just then, Stacy heard yelling coming from the conference room. "Oh boy, here we go," she grumbled under her breath.

Taking a deep breath before she slowly pushed open the glass door to the executive board room, she put the best fake smile on her face and said calmly, "Good morning, ladies and gentlemen." As she entered, she knew she had to think quickly on her feet. *Come on, Stacy, you can do it. No one must know he's not coming.*

TRACY ANNE BERTINI

The tall, thin man hovering over the corner table next to the window that looked out over the entire city quickly turned toward her greeting. His eyes were stern and dark and had a heavy brow, not friendly at all. Sebastian was not a man to disappoint. He stood with authority and, as usual, was impeccably dressed in his custom European suit. Everyone in the room was unnerved with his presence. Everyone quickly sat in their seats as Sebastian stared back out the window and said in a breathy, deep-toned voice, "Where the hell is he? Someone better have an answer for me right now! I will not be disrespected. My time is precious, and I will not wait for my update."

Stacy slowly and timidly raised her hand and said, "I am sorry, sir. I have contacted Mike, and well, umm, he is very sick, but I do have all the status reports right here."

Before she could even get the rest of her words out, he slammed his fist on the mahogany table and yelled, "This is unacceptable!" He reached in his coat pocket, pulled out his cell phone, and quickly sent a message. As they all sat there ready to receive what they could only imagine would be the worst tongue-lashing any of them would ever hear, Sebastian swiftly grabbed his briefcase and, without another word, left not only the boardroom but also the building. He jumped into the black sedan waiting out front. The car sped off and quickly entered the freeway heading north out of the city.

Mike had taken this job to advise and oversee the project. He was a chef by trade and wanted to help the local farmers with the lack of water. His passion has always been using fresh, organic, locally grown ingredients.

He grew up in a small town in the Midwest as the son of a local farmer. Every morning before school, he would complete his chores around the farm; he would feed the chickens, cows, and pigs. He often sat there and wondered how to help the local farmers. Every day, he witnessed the efforts of his family and how the lack of rain did affect each household. How could he not want to help?

He was a mild-mannered boy growing up with a great sense of humor and work ethic. He excelled in science and sports in school. Even with the never-ending farmwork, his father was always present at all his sporting events. As the years went by, Mike slowly watched his father age; the work was too much for him now. His father sadly said that it was time to sell the farm.

Mike was working at a local restaurant when he first met Sebastian, after he continually complained about everything during his visit that day. Of course, Sebastian always did his homework, handpicking Mike for just that reason. It was not by chance he chose this restaurant and this town. He needed the local farmers on board with his plan and needed Mike's credibility so they would not ask any questions with all the comings and goings in the small rural town located in the Rockies in a valley north of Denver. The townspeople mostly kept to themselves but were very friendly; a smile and good-morning were standard greetings. Sebastian had this area under surveillance for a few years now. He felt it was the perfect place to implement his plan.

As Mike entered the diner for his usual breakfast, he stopped to look at his beloved mountains; since he moved here after the sale of the farm, he loved the peace the small town in the valley provided. Joe, the owner of the diner, greeted him. He was a handsome man with boyish good looks and a sarcastic nature. He opened Joe's Diner about eight years ago after relocating here. He grew up in Boston. The local townsfolk could hardly understand him at times as he never lost his accent. The diner displays his most precious sports memorabilia from his Boston teams. He caught a lot of crap from the locals at times, but being stubborn and a true Yankee, he refused to cave in to the pressure. Mike and Joe had become friends almost instantly.

"Morning, Mike. The usual?" Joe asked.

He replied, "Yup, sounds like a plan."

Joe continued while he poured hot, freshly brewed coffee into the cup on the counter. "So how about the weather? It's been crazy this year."

Mike replied, "Huh? Oh yeah, right."

Joe could tell Mike was distracted generally; by now, they were picking on each other's teams and throwing insults while laughing. Finally, about ten minutes into the routine, Joe stopped and said, "Hey, Mike, seriously, you OK, man?" Mike didn't even respond.

Just then, the phone rang. Joe shook his head in confusion and went to the back to answer the ringing phone. "'Morning. Joe's Diner," he said to the person on the other line. The voice asked if he had seen Mike, and before Joe could say he was in there, Mike was gone.

Well, that was different, Joe thought. Before he could put much more thought into it, he noticed more customers sitting down. *Hmm, I'll call him later.* Joe noticed that, since Mike took on this new advising job, he had been easily distracted and busy on most days.

Back at the cabin, Anya had just finished her omelet and was washing the dishes in the sun-drenched kitchen. *So what's on the agenda today?* she thought. Going to the local home improvement store was a must so Anya could finally finish her renovation of the cabin, and of course, she was having lunch in town.

She grew up in Burlington, Massachusetts, with her mother, sister, and brother. Her mother worked to provide for the family. Anya spent her summers with her grandmother at the cabin in the North Georgia mountains.

Her grandmother was very fond of a small Bavarian town called Helen. It made her feel at home, especially when she was missing Germany. They would often take the twenty-minute drive to Helen. They would eat lunch at one of the local German restaurants. Sonya always cherished her German roots and loved to drink German beer and eat sauerkraut and bratwurst. During lunch, they would talk about life. Anya loved the thick German accent her grandmother had. It was comforting, like a warm hug. Sonya had many funny stories of her childhood. It was happy and filled with music, laughter, and food in the mountain region of Germany. Growing up, Sonya would always braid Anya's hair in Bavarian-style braids and would dress her in dirndls, which Anya loved.

As Anya got changed and ready to head out toward town, the weather radio went off and said that there was a tornado warning for her area. *Well, I guess I'll postpone my trip for a few hours and let the storm pass*, she thought. Anya went back upstairs to grab a book and her afghan that her grandmother had crocheted for her. It was a family tradition that Sonya would always crochet afghans and, of course, bake her Christmas cookies. Her grandmother was very traditional.

She walked to her screened porch off the master bedroom and decided she would watch the storm from there. She lit a fire in the stacked stone fireplace. Then settled into the chaise lounge with her coffee refill, book and afghan in hand. As she sat, she exhaled. *Now that's what I'm talking about*, she thought. She could smell the fresh rain in the distance as she heard the gentle roll of thunder against the mountains; it was always soothing to her, even as a young child.

It was about the time when Joe would start his routine of closing the diner—first, the dishes, the counters, and the floors; and then he would prep for the next day. He enjoyed his work. Halfway through his prep, he remembered his strange encounter with Mike earlier that day, so he pulled out his phone and dialed his number. It went right to his voice mail. "Hey, this is Mike. You missed me. Leave a message. I'll call you back."

So Joe left a message. "Hey, man, just checking up on you. You seemed distracted this morning, and you got me a little worried. Let's get some beers to take your mind off the stress of the job tonight. Give me a call. Talk to you soon." Joe and Mike would often meet at a local brewery to put back a few beers and talk shit about their day; it was a great way to end their day and blow off steam.

The bartender at the bar was a fascinating guy, originally from California; he was always talking about some type of conspiracy theory. The locals didn't pay much attention to old Buzz, a Vietnam vet who was highly suspicious of everyone and everything; he was kind enough. He would tell anyone who would listen about how our government has been experimenting on us guinea pigs since George Washington's days. Of course, old Buzz had just enough factual information to draw you into his stories and then would always end with "Well, you don't have to listen to old Buzz. What the hell do I know anyway?" Buzz got drafted during the Vietnam War as a high school senior. He got his nickname because he would always get buzzed after the game, so the name just stuck.

His girlfriend since middle school was a sweet, shy girl named Julianna Faith Thompson. Everyone called her Faith, probably because her dad was the town pastor at the local church. Their family was the typical churchgoing family, always willing to help out people in need, and their doors were always open. Pastor Thompson was a middle-aged man with salt-and-pepper hair and the biggest heart you'd ever meet. His wife, Cindy, was the best apple pie baker in this side of the Mississippi. The Thompson family loved Buzz and always welcomed him as their son.

Buzz grew up in a broken home and often stayed on friends' couches after passing out. His father left when he was only two, never to have been heard from again. Although Pastor and Cindy did not agree with Buzz's drinking, they were there for him no matter what. Pastor Thompson was present at every Friday night football game to support his "son."

The town always just expected Faith and Buzz would marry right out of high school, buy a house in the area, and start a family. The American dream was what everyone strove to achieve. Buzz adored Faith, and it was apparent to everyone in the town. That kind of love is a once-in-a-lifetime gift. They met in sixth grade at the Sadie Hawkins Day dance; Faith was too shy to ask a boy to the social, so there she sat in the corner in her brand-new purple dress. Buzz walked in, goofing around with his friends, and stopped to notice her sitting there with a smile on her face. He knew he had to go and talk to her.

"Hey, Faith, who did you ask to the dance?" Faith's cheeks turned a bright reddish pink.

"Oh well, I didn't ask anyone, Buzz. Did you come with someone?" she said as she slightly swayed back and forth and twirled her hair.

"Nope, no way!" he quickly responded. Then he realized he didn't actually mean to be that forward. "Oh, I mean, well, no, the girl that I like, well, um, you didn't ask."

"Well, Buzz, would you escort me to the Sadie Hawkins dance tonight? I know it's late, and we are already here, but I would love to hang out with you." Buzz placed her hand in his, and they walked toward the dance floor.

CHAPTER TWO

EVERYTHING WOULD CHANGE for Buzz and Faith three months before graduation. Faith and Buzz hiked to their favorite spot and had been talking for hours about their plans after school got out. They had planned to take a road trip down the old Route 66 and see the country as their honeymoon adventure. Faith always laid her head on Buzz's lap as he gently brushed her hair between his fingers. It was how they had spent many afternoons together over the last four years.

Buzz had been saving to buy a car for their trip; he had his eye on a sweet 1955 candy-apple red Chevy Corvette convertible. He would talk for hours about that car, from the whitewall tires to the smoothly rounded headlights; it was his dream car. Mr. Richardson owned the local garage and had allowed Buzz to come and work in there in exchange for the car, and in his spare time, he continued to restore his Corvette.

Faith helped Cindy every Sunday at church as a Sunday school teacher for the toddlers; she loved those bright-eyed little ones. You would often find her under the pile of children on the story-time rug in the toddler room. Buzz and Faith had decided they would have six children when they got married. The wedding plans were just starting to come together, and of course, Pastor Thompson was honored to officiate the ceremony. Cindy had given Faith the very wedding gown she wore when she exchanged vows over thirty years ago with her father. The wedding would be such a big event for the whole town. A Saturday in September would be their special day.

Later that evening, Buzz walked Faith home. Cindy asked him to stay for dinner, which had become a tradition, but Buzz declined her invitation today. He gave Faith a kiss goodbye and held her as she rested her head on his chest and listened to his heartbeat. They embraced for what seemed like forever. Buzz dropped his hands, slowly pulled his hand from Faith's grasp, and said, "I love you. I'll be here in the morning." He would always walk to her house on his way to school, and they would then walk hand in hand the rest of the way.

Buzz arrived just like clockwork that day at 7:25 a.m. As they walked, Faith could tell something was on Buzz's mind. In the distance, they could hear the warning bell, which always rang at precisely 7:55 a.m. to let all the students and staff know they had ten minutes till the first period would start. Just before they arrived at the front door, Faith asked Buzz, "What was wrong?"

He told her, "Oh, nothing, just thinking."

While in math class, Buzz heard the news footage coming from the faculty lounge next door. He couldn't help but hear about the war and all the casualties that were happening overseas. He often wondered if he should go and fight for his country, but that had already been decided for him.

Later that night, he drove to Faith's house; and as he knocked on the door, Pastor Thompson greeted him with a warm smile. "Well, hey there, Buzz. How's life treating you tonight?" he asked.

"Well, sir, it is great. Thank you for asking. And you?" Buzz answered.

Pastor Thompson replied with a smile, "Just fine, son, and happy to hear it. So I hear we have some vows to write. There is no way I'll let my little girl's special day be anything but perfect. I'm here to help if you need it, Buzz. I hope you know that. You are the son I never had, and each day I thank God for your being in our lives."

As they walked through the living room, the phone suddenly rang from the kitchen, where Cindy was once again preparing a family meal for the Thompsons. The voice on the other line asked to speak with Mr. Thompson; she handed the phone to him as she brought the casserole dish to the old farm table in the corner of the kitchen.

As they waited for Mr. Thompson to finish up his phone call, they sat patiently. Buzz and Faith were discussing their plans for the honeymoon as he boasted about his Corvette being just about finished. "Finally, after all this time!"

About fifteen minutes after the phone rang, Pastor Thompson came to the dinner table, and he had a sad and concerned look on his face. He was not good at hiding his emotions, and Cindy knew something was troubling him. She asked him to please sit and say grace so the family could eat before the meal got cold.

After their dinner and light conversation, Pastor Thompson asked Buzz to take a walk out back to the old family barn. This was a stroll the two had shared many times. Pastor Thompson sat on the old wooden rocking chair and motioned for Buzz to sit on the other. As they both looked up to the stars, Pastor said, "Ya know, Buzz, sometimes in our lives, we are called to do amazing things, and we don't always agree or understand, but we do it anyway. Son, this is one of these times. The call I received was from the deacon at the church who also was the local army recruiting officer. Sam said you've been drafted, son. You'll be heading to war by week's end."

Sebastian's father had his nightly routine; after returning home for the day, he would take off his expensive suit coat and slip on his smoking jacket, grab the bottle of brandy and a cigar, and retire to the library. There wasn't much time for Sebastian. As a boy, he would spend many hours outside the tall oak door of the library, imagining what was going on in there.

On Thursday nights, ten other gentlemen would join Sebastian's father in his nightly ritual. He would refer to them, under his breath, as the masters of the universe. Each of them impeccably dressed— politicians, millionaires, renowned physicians, and even a well-known actor. New money and old money was mixed in the group. Sebastian could not figure out what the tie between these men was. He knew he could not speak to any of the men; he was ordered just to open the door and show them to the library.

Their home was an enormous estate surrounded by mature landscaping, large trees, and a lake. The property reached across fifty acres and was strategically located just outside the Denver International Airport. With his ear on the heavy door to the library, Sebastian could only hear low, muted, almost grumbled voices, which frustrated him. Oh how he longed to know what they were saying to one another.

Sebastian's father, Johnathon Alexander Tutworth III, was a strange man; he stood about six feet five inches and had a medium build. His jet-black hair was perfectly coiffed back with not a hair out of place. His chiseled jawline would never have a hair on it, cleanly shaven only. Johnathon was a playboy of sorts; ever since Sebastian's mother passed away when he was six years old, you would often see a young starlet on Johnathon's arm night after night.

The au pair for Sebastian was Ms. Charlotte; she was born and raised in South Carolina and was just as sweet as can be. He would often hear his father yelling at her, "Stop letting Sebastian have free time! Idle time is no good. The boy must keep to his studies. I will not have complacency under my roof. I will not tolerate mediocrity."

Nothing about the Tutworths was average, from homes to vehicles, educations, vacations, and of course the parties. Only the finest things were selected for their home. The draperies and linens of exquisite silks were imported from Persia. The artworks that adorned the walls in the grand entryway were from both local and international artists.

Johnathon had impeccable tastes and extremely high standards. His voice would bellow through the halls as he would yell at Sebastian, "Stand up straight like a man!" Sebastian walked with a slight hunch in his back and was a very peculiar child; his dark bangs would always fall in front of his eyes, which drove his father mad. He did not fit in at school with his classmates; he was much shorter and thinner than the boys his age.

Often at night, you would hear Johnathon grumbling under his breath, "How could Sebastian be such a disappointment? He can't be my son. I will not tolerate laziness. How can he be so lazy that he can't stand up straight?" Jonathon shook his head and slammed his fist on the table that held the brandy. He would then pour a glass, slam the heavy oak door to the library, and be gone just as fast as a summer thunderstorm.

All Sebastian had ever wanted was his father's approval or even to be noticed by him as not a disappointment but someone worthy of his father's legacy. Although he was not handsome or athletic, he had already started acquiring his sharp negotiation skills. The other boys would try to bully him into doing their assignments for school; he would agree and then use it to his advantage to stop the other kids from bullying or humiliating him. Sebastian was actually quite brilliant and had mastered the art of the deal.

CHAPTER THREE

A S THE THUNDER started to let up, Anya heard a noise that startled her. *What was that?* she thought as she rubbed her eyes, realizing she must've fallen asleep. She stood up and looked out the window as she lovingly folded the afghan and placed it back into Sonya's hope chest at the foot of the large four-poster bed.

Going into the bathroom to splash some cold water on her face to help her awake from her afternoon snooze, she walked in front of the mirror hanging on the wall; she stopped as she noticed a small fog or smudge on the bottom right of the mirror. *I guess I didn't clean it as well as I thought. That reminds me to pick up a window cleaner while I'm out.* Grabbing a baseball hat from the closet, she threw her hair up in a loose ponytail and started down the stairs.

Entering the kitchen, she noticed that the back door had what looked like two wet footprints perfectly placed on the floor. *OK, now that is weird*, she thought. *Had someone come in while I was sleeping? Nah, I was way out in the middle of nowhere in the mountains. The rain must have leaked in under the door and just happened to settle in two puddles that resemble footprints.* Anya would always walk and talk her way through things logically. *Yes, that is what happened. OK, add a new weather strip for the door.*

She grabbed her keys, popped on the outside light switch for the front porch, jumped into her four-wheel-drive jeep, and headed down the dirt and gravel road for the almost-fifteen-mile-ride to an actual paved road. She rolled down the windows once she had reached the paved road, and she turned up her tunes; she loved driving with the windows down and music on and feeling the cold, crisp air of the fall in Georgia.

On her trip to town, she passed several farm stands and apple orchards, as well as the many vineyards that had popped up in the area over the last ten years. The scenery was tranquil in this part of the state; the rolling green hills and open pastures were plenty. She would reflect fondly on her many drives to town with her grandmother.

As she pulled up to the home improvement store, she noticed one of the local farmers; he would always bring his fresh produce, jams, and honey to the local farmers market every week. She warmly greeted him with a "Good afternoon," to which he replied, "'Afternoon to you, ma'am."

As they made small talk about the storms that just came through, he informed her he was most thankful for the rain as it has been unusually dry this year, and the crops definitely suffered. In fact, he was worried about the loss of income this year and his projection for next year's crops. "It's not looking good," he said with a sigh. "'Haven't seen it this dry since I was a boy. This weather is just crazy. I'm fixin' to head down yonder and talk to the director of the water department and see if I can get some water delivered." The local economy, like so many others in small towns, depended on the rain for their crops to support their families. The farms in this area have been here since the plantations and handed down from generation to generation. The people in North Georgia were hardworking, honest, and just about as friendly as anyone could be—neighbor helping a fellow neighbor and taking pride in their community.

There was a man-made reservoir not too far from here, but even Lake Lanier was dangerously low this year. Anya spent many summer days at the lake boating with friends on her visits to the mountains. Lake Lanier had become very busy with boaters, Jet Skiers, and swimmers. Even that didn't happen this year; many people had to give up as their docks were stranded, and the land all around was dry and cracked. It was quite the sight to see—the red Georgia clay parched for miles, looking like a desert. The locals also depended on the lake and summer activities for their livelihood; without the lake being usable, the local economy was in danger.

Anya walked inside the store to get her supplies. While in the middle aisle looking for the glass cleaner, she felt as if someone were watching her; she began to feel uneasy as if she could feel the eyes piercing into her very soul. She breathed in and spun around to see who was there. *That is so strange*, she thought. *Oh, Anya, stop letting your imagination get the best of you.*

Leaving the store, she caught a glimpse of a strange car speeding up from the parking lot and heading east. She noticed the time and decided it was time to head back to the cabin before it got dark. There were no streetlights once you left the paved road, just the stars to light your way. As she turned right to enter the old dirt road, she could've sworn she saw faint lights coming from the road about a quarter mile in; as she blinked to adjust her sight, they were gone. Again, she thought, *What a strange day I had!*

Grabbing her bags from the jeep, she unlocked the door, entered the kitchen, and put the bags on the counter. Anya was tired and headed up to the bathroom to take a hot bath and read a book she had just started; as she headed upstairs, she remembered she needed to clean the smudge from the mirror. *I almost forgot to grab the window cleaner*, she thought, shaking her head. She grabbed the bottle and headed upstairs. She picked up her book, poured a glass of wine, and started the hot bath.

As she undressed, she walked toward the mirror and stopped abruptly. The smudge was gone. *Where could it have gone? It was there this morning.* She wanted just to be finished with today. Anya did have an issue with her memory at times since her accident, especially when she was tired or stressed. She settled into the hot bath, sipped on her wine, and started into chapter 3 as she thought, *It's getting good now, and I can't wait to see what happens next.*

Joe was locking up for the day and walking to his car when he noticed large tire tracks in the snow in the alley behind the diner. He thought, *Hmm, strange. From the looks of the tracks, someone was definitely in a hurry.* Joe drove over to the brewery to meet Mike. When he walked in, Buzz greeted him loudly as the game was playing on the TVs; and of course, everyone was cheering their team on.

"Hey, Joe, what can I get you? Where's Mike at? I haven't seen him much since he started doing that job with that weird suit guy."

Joe laughed. "Yeah, that suit guy is an ass. I don't know how Mike puts up with him. The paycheck better be worth it."

Buzz replied, "He's not just an ass but also weird. I don't know. I think there's more to that story. 'Kinda reminds me of a typical government guy, CIA or FBI. I mean, he's been sneaking around here for months in his fancy cars, and he's always on the phone, like he's that important. I am just saying he's up to no good, but don't listen to old Buzz." Then they both finished with "What the hell do I know anyway?" as they laughed together.

Joe ordered some wings and his favorite stout from the tap. Buzz said, "All righty, I'll put it in, buddy. Give me, like, fifteen minutes." He then left the bar area and headed to the kitchen, noticing the back door was wide open. "Son of a bitch, I'm not paying to heat all of friggin' Dillon." He slammed the door, shook his head, and walked away.

When the order was ready, Buzz placed it on the bar in front of Joe, who now was fully involved in the game. Joe looked away for just a second to thank him for the wings and request some blue cheese. "Oh right, why the hell do I always forget the blue cheese? My shitty memory, I guess, or maybe it's the Agent Orange from 'Nam." He would often refer to the crazy things he believed the government was doing to the soldiers during wartime. Buzz also had thoughts of conspiracy about drive-thrus and the local dry cleaner. Everyone in town cut him some slack; he had been through so much in his life.

While he was away in Vietnam, his fiancée had been killed in a massive highway pileup; he was never the same after that. Rumor was she was carrying their first child. The drinking had become his way of numbing the pain after that. He moved here to get away from the ghosts and memories that haunted him of the life he was supposed to have with Faith.

Buzz came back from the kitchen and had a puzzled look on his face. "What's up, Buzz?" Joe asked as he was wiping the wing sauce from his cheek.

TRACY ANNE BERTINI

"So a few minutes ago, I noticed the back door was open, so I slammed it good. Then I came out here and went back to get the blue cheese, and it was open again. They are watching us. I'm telling you, Joe, they are always watching."

Joe put his hand on Buzz's shoulder and said, "It's all right, buddy. The more customers who come in, the better for your wallet, right?"

Buzz asked Joe if he could just keep his eye on the rookie bartender; he needed to take a break. "Of course, Buzz, go chill for a bit," Joe said. "Besides, I'm still waiting for Mike unless, of course, I'm getting stood up."

CHAPTER FOUR

W HEN MIKE WOKE up, he realized he had no idea what had happened; he looked around to try to get his bearings. *Where the hell am I, and what just happened? I was at the diner talking to Joe and then . . . blank.* He stood up, steadied himself, and walked down the hall toward a brightly lighted room; he could hear voices coming from it. Nothing looked familiar.

As he walked through the door, he saw Stacy, his secretary, sitting there. The talking abruptly stopped, and she jumped up and said, "Oh thank god, Mike. We were worried. How do you feel? You were quite sick for a while there."

Mike replied, "I have no idea what happened. Do you? How long was I out, and where the hell are we?"

She replied, "Well, you need to sit down. I have something to tell you, but first, you need to eat something. You're going to need your strength." Stacy quickly headed to the fridge, grabbed a pouchlike small package from the refrigerator, and handed it to Mike. "Here, eat."

He looked at the strange box and asked, "What is it?"

She said sternly, "Mike, we don't have time. Just eat. We have to leave as soon as your strength allows. They are only one step behind us. Please, Mike, eat!"

Mike was starting to feel hungry. *OK,* he thought. *There will be plenty of time for explanations after I ate.* Looking at the package, he noticed the writing on it was his. "Stacy, why is my writing on this box?" He had a confused sort of voice.

"Oh, you don't remember anything? That's far worse than you had thought. Eat and rest. We need to leave by daylight."

Mike was surprised at the taste of this unique package, so he asked, "Where did you get this?"

She replied, "I listened to your message, went to the freezer at your house, and packed up everything on the list you sent."

"What? Wait, a list? Stacy, I didn't send you a list. What the hell is going on?"

"I have no idea," she replied. "I received the list via your e-mail ten days ago when you didn't show up for the meeting with Sebastian. I followed your instructions, and then three days ago, I arrived here using your coordinates in the e-mail, and here you were, asleep. You were hooked up to a heart monitor, and your vitals were stable. In fact, the nurse said you were going to be just fine, that they were giving fluids to you only as a precaution."

"I need to lie down, Stacy. Where is the room I stayed in?"

She showed him the way to the chamber, but she stopped dead in her tracks. "There were all kinds of medical supplies and machines in here. Where did they go?"

"Let's call it a night. We need to rest if we are going to leave in the a.m., like you said."

"OK, Mike. 'Night. We have a lot to talk about tomorrow."

Sebastian had arrived in record time; as the driver pulled the sedan into the five-car garage, Sebastian asked, "Is it done?"

The driver replied, "Yes, sir. Every last detail has been taken care of per your request."

"Good! We must not stray from the plan. Not one little detail will change. The fate of my father's lifework depends on it, and I will not let him down."

"Yes, sir, I understand. Can I do anything else for you tonight?"

"No," he abruptly said. "Just leave me to my work. Do not allow anyone to disturb me!"

Sebastian flung open the library door and headed toward the brandy, just as his father had done many times before him. Taking a sip from the glass, he turned and looked at the formal painting of his father and said, "Father, we are so close. I wish you were here to see how your work is being carried out. I have spared no expense and left no stone unturned. It is like watching a beautiful play or listening to our favorite symphony as our senses hang on every note, and it rushes over our body like a seductive massage. Sonya will regret everything! I will make them all pay, Father. That is my solemn vow to you. It is time, Father, for the next step. As we speak, all the chess pieces are in place!"

Just then, he started to sway as the music began to play from the old record player located on the bookshelf. Dancing around the room in a waltz-type pattern, he was extremely proud of himself; he had done it! Sebastian seemed to be somewhere else now, with the music getting louder and darker.

Then there was a knock at the door; he stopped and walked to the record player, ending the music abruptly. As he opened the door, he took a large breath as he opened his mouth, about to yell at the person on the other side; but he quickly stopped, ran his hands through his hair to collect himself, and calmly said, "Oh, it's you. I wasn't expecting you. Please come in."

The hot bath had made Anya sleepy; she was having difficulty reading her book, and then she gently fell asleep. Anya would soak for hours, just replacing the water as needed to keep the temp just right. She stepped out onto the bath mat and grabbed her robe off the hook behind the door. *I am exhausted*, she thought as she pulled back the sheets and slipped into bed for the night.

As the sun came up over the mountains, Anya started to stir. Stretching her arms out of the warm bed, she yawned and stepped onto the floor. As every morning before she started her routine, she sipped her coffee while walking out the porch. Looking toward the rose garden, she noticed the dew was not on the roses as it normally would. *Why is that?* she thought. Then she had a flashback to a day of gardening with her grandmother, who told her in that night's story to always look at the morning dew; it should be a perfect blanket across the grass and flowers. Her grandmother's stories were always fun and practical.

Hmm, she thought. *So who or what had been here this morning before I awoke?* Anya stepped down into the yard and quickly noticed footsteps next to the rose bushes. They appeared to be the same size as the rain-soaked ones from yesterday at the back door. *What is going on?*

Just then, she heard a loud crash coming from inside. She ran back inside to see the kitchen all disheveled, drawers all open, everything everywhere. She reached for her phone and dialed 911. "White County 911. What's your emergency?"

"Yes, my name is Anya, and someone has broken into my house. I need help quick!"

"OK, ma'am, please stay on the line until you hear the sirens approaching the house. Are you in a safe location? Is the intruder still in the house with you?" As Anya started to explain what had happened, she noticed something bizarre; there was a piece of paper of some sort hanging from the bottom of one of the overturned drawers. She walked over to it and took hold of it; just then, the whole bottom of the drawer fell out onto the floor. The voice on the other line was now louder. "Ma'am, are you still there? Ma'am!"

Anya quickly responded, "Yes, I'm still here. Sorry, I am just so overwhelmed."

She thought, *Who would do this?*

Just about then, Anya heard the sirens coming down the old dirt road. "I can hear them," she told the 911 dispatcher.

"OK, ma'am, hold on just a minute. Can you safely get to the front door to unlock it for the officers?" Anya said yes and quickly walked to the front door to open it just as the officers walked up the stairs to the porch.

The sun was just starting to rise over the Rocky Mountains as Mike awoke. He quickly thought, *We have to leave*, as he yelled for Stacy. He jumped out of bed, threw on his pants and shirt, and started to reach for his watch that he placed on the table. *But wait, where was the table?*

"Stacy!" he yelled even louder. He spun around and realized he was in his bedroom at what seemed to be his house. *Was that all a crazy dream? What happened?* He noticed the time and decided he was going to wash up, and he was in desperate need of coffee.

Walking down stairs to the kitchen, he kept reliving the events from the night before; it was so real, but could it have been a dream? He filled his cup and sat down. *I better write this down. It was too strange and felt too real.* In fact, it had him pretty shaken. He started typing away on his tablet feverishly as he recalled as many details as he could. It was Wednesday according to the calendar, so he had to head to the restaurant.

Driving toward Denver today felt different; it was the commute he made every morning for years now, but it just felt different. As he entered the kitchen at the restaurant, he was greeted by the kitchen staff. "Hey, Mike, how's it going, man?" Walking into the office, he saw the stats of sales and customer satisfaction; they all looked good. His desk looked normal, nothing out of place. The time was about nine by now, and every morning, he would meet with his staff, go over things for the day, and discuss new recipe ideas, just the general state of stuff there.

Mike's staff adored and respected him. He was friendly and genuinely cared about all the people in his life. He started the meeting with "So does anyone have any good news or anything you want to talk about?" Nothing was out of the ordinary today, same old stuff. The meeting was status quo; he decided to head back to his office and work on his admin stuff.

Every so often, he would stare off in what seemed to be a daydream. "Mike, Mike, are you even listening to me, man?" Joe stood in the doorway to the office and finally put his hand on Mike's shoulder. Mike jumped as if he had no idea Joe had been standing there for over four minutes, talking.

"Joe, oh man, I didn't see you there."

"Well, I guess you just have a lot on your mind," Joe replied. "I was just coming by for some of the new tomatoes you grew in your garden. I have an idea for a new southwestern omelet."

"Oh, right, they are on the prep table in the kitchen. Just grab some, hey, and let me know what you think."

Joe headed to the table and grabbed the tomatoes, and as he was leaving, he stuck his head back in and said, "You know you missed one hell of a game last night. I waited at the brewery for a little bit. Well, anyway, Mike, you coming tonight? Round 2 of the playoffs?" Mike raised his hand and gave him a thumbs-up.

That day was completely uneventful. As they were cleaning up the lunch rush, Mike noticed his phone was completely dead, so he

TRACY ANNE BERTINI

rummaged through his desk drawer and found his charger. While the phone was charging, he would try to call Stacy; she was his secretary for the project he has been advising on, but he considered them friends. Her phone went to voice mail, which just didn't happen ever. He had been working with her on the project for three years now, and never did it go to voice mail. "Hey, Stacy, it's Mike. Give me a call when you get this. 'Just wanted to know what suggestions the team had for this week's testing and to make sure we are on track for Mr. Tutworth's time line. 'Talk to you soon. Oh, and seeing as I'm getting your voice mail, I hope you are enjoying some time to yourself."

CHAPTER FIVE

AFTER THE POLICE had asked Anya many questions, they told her the report would be available in about twenty-four hours but that, if she needed anything, she shouldn't hesitate to call. The officer handed her his card. "Thank you for all your help today, and I will have a good day, Officer." Anya followed them to the front door and locked it behind them.

She turned to the huge mess now left for her to clean up. *Well, I better get started on this mess.* She grabbed a bag and began the task of cleaning the clutter left by the intruder. With this mess, it could have been *intruders*; the very thought of anyone violating her sanctuary shook her to her core. Anya said out loud, "I mean, I would've given you what you wanted anyway, so I don't understand why!" She decided to make piles of things to go through to try to speed it up.

She heard a knock at the door; it was her friend Jess. They had been friends for twelve years now; ironically, they were both from New England. Jess and Anya had hit it off immediately. "Wow, what a mess! I heard what happened while I was at the grocery store this morning. Why didn't you call?"

"I would've, but I called 911, and they were here for what seemed like forever, so I figured I would just call you later."

Jess walked to the counter and made them both a cup of coffee, placed them on the table, and said, "Well, let's get to work."

As they sat on the floor sifting through the mounds of papers, Anya looked toward the overturned drawer leaning against the refrigerator. "Jess, what is that stuck to the bottom of that drawer?"

Jess quickly looked at the drawer and gently pulled off what looked like a brochure of sorts. "I'm not sure. It looks ancient and yellow. The writing is all faded from the front of it."

Anya put her hand out to reach for the brochure. "Here, let me take a look." As she reached for the pamphlet, she noticed something peculiar, a symbol on the front. She had definitely seen this symbol many times. It was in the stained-glass window at the cabin that she had stared at many times as she felt the warmth of the sun under her feet. *What a strange coincidence*, she thought. "Jess, come here and take a look at this."

They both walked over to the stained glass. The sun was shining in through the window, and they both noticed the sand dollar design in the middle. This had always been Anya's favorite part of the window, but today she saw something different: in tiny writing on one of the edges, there was the number 333 with the letters SGD. They both stood there looking at it and wondering what that was. "Anya, do you think it is the artist's initials?" Jess asked.

"I really have no idea what it means." Then Anya held up the brochure in front of the window and noticed the same numbers and letters in the sand dollar when the sun shone through the paper; she quickly took it down from the sunlight, and it was gone. Several times, they held it up and down to see.

"Wow, Anya, that is kind of cool. I read something one time about secret messages on paper that only direct light would show. What else is in on the brochure?" Jess inquired. Looking at the old brochure, the only other thing that Anya could make out was the word guide and part of a black-and-white photo of what looked like pillars. "After we clean up this mess, we should go to the library and see if there is any info we can find on the artist who created the stained-glass window."

"Sounds like a plan. We can grab a bite to eat while we are out. I'm starving, and it has been a long day. Well, that about does it. I can finish the rest tomorrow." Anya turned around as Jess had not replied. "Jess? Jess, where did you go?" She walked around the corner to see Jess just standing there staring at the back door, where there was a note tacked to it.

"Anya, did you see this?"

"See what?" she replied.

"This note right here on the door."

Anya quickly walked over to Jess, and they both read it out loud. "We are always watching while you are awake, while you are sleeping. Till we meet again."

"Wait, that wasn't there a few minutes ago. Where did it come from, and who is watching? Anya, let's bring this to the police, and I think you should stay at my house tonight."

"I appreciate it, Jess, but the officers were here for several hours. They could not find anything. I'm safe. In fact, I'm going to take a rain check on the trip to the library. I'm just going to call for some takeout. You are more than welcome to stay, Jess."

"Let me run out, and I'll pick us up food. Are you sure you're OK for a few? I'll bring this note to the sheriff's office while I'm out."

Anya placed her hand on Jess's shoulder and said, "Thank you. I'll see you when you get back. Oh hey, Jess, grab some extra duck sauce too."

"You bet," said Jess as she headed out the front door.

The sun was just starting to set over the mountains. Anya pulled out her laptop and googled stained-glass artists in the time period the cabin was built; she found nothing. It was times like this she really wished her grandmother were here to comfort her and give her advice. She sat on the couch in the living room and put on the television for a few minutes to get her mind off everything that had transpired today. She walked to the kitchen pantry to pull out paper plates as she was expecting Jess to return any minute.

Just then, she heard the newscaster. "We have a breaking story. The CDC confirms over twenty cases of a rare flu-like illness that causes dementia-like symptoms. Three deaths have been confirmed in the outskirts of Denver."

"The cases have been tracked in Colorado and Georgia," said Spokeswoman Hardy from the CDC. "There is no reason to panic as these cases seemed to be isolated, and we are working diligently with local physicians and our research department heads to analyze data from our teams in both states."

"Oh boy, here we go again with another flu virus. The lines at the clinic will be ridiculous for the flu shot this year," Anya said.

Jess finally arrived back with their takeout; they both sat and enjoyed their impromptu girl's night. "So the sheriff said they think it was some local teens just trying to scare you, but they will continue to look into it, and if anything changes, call them," Jess explained.

"Thanks for doing that. I was so tired of telling the story and answering the same questions over and over again."

"What are friends for anyway? I got you, girl," Jess said with a smile. "Anya, did you find anything about the stained-glass artist?"

"Actually," Anya said, "it seems as if no one made it."

"What? I mean, it's here, so someone had to have done it." Jess laughed.

"That's weird, but you know how the old paper records are up here in the country," Anya said as she shook her head. "I made up the guest room for you. Do you need anything else before I head up?"

"No, I'm good." Jess smiled.

"All right then, good night."

"'Night," Jess replied.

Anya turned and walked up the stairs, down the hall, and into her room. As she walked across the floor to her bed, she thought, *What a long day.*

"Time to say goodbye to today. Tomorrow would be another day," she said with a smile. It was how her grandmother would tuck her every night.

Mike walked into the brewery as Joe motioned him over. "Hey, buddy, you actually made it. Buzz, get the man a beer!" Joe yelled.

"So our team's down but hopefully not for long. I ordered nachos. Have some. Buzz said it's a new recipe he came up with while he was meditating this morning, but don't ask him what's in them. I think it's better if we don't know."

Mike agreed. "All right, man, nachos it is. Hey, Buzz, can we get another round?"

Buzz nodded. "Coming right up." He walked back to the bar and filled a pitcher with beer for the guys.

"So, Mike, what happened last night, man? I waited, left messages, and texted you. Still fighting that bug you had?" Joe asked.

"Nah, I think I fell asleep and had one hell of a dream. Have you ever had one of those dreams that feel so real you swore they were real? Last night, I had one of those dreams, but I can't believe it wasn't real," Mike explained. "Last thing I remember, I was talking to you at the diner, and then I woke up in this weird room surrounded by medical equipment, and I could hear faint voices coming from down the hall. So of course, I followed them. As soon as I walked into the room, it went silent. Two men were talking to Stacy. When they saw me, they quickly left out the front door. Stacy said that I sent her an e-mail, like, ten days ago, I missed a meeting for the project, and I gave her specific plans to follow. That's how she found me, wherever I was. I remember being so tired and weak that I just wanted to sleep. She mentioned something about a nurse and fluids or something like that. It's a little hazy now. Oh, I do remember eating something and then walking back to the room where I woke up, and all the medical equipment was gone. Even Stacy noticed it, but then I woke up in my room at home."

Buzz couldn't help but hear Mike's strange dream. "You know, Mike, we haven't heard from you in about ten days. Come to think of it. Do you recall anything else about the dream?" Buzz chimed in.

"I mean, kind of, but it's all a big jumble of snapshot of memories," Mike replied.

Buzz then asked, "What about any changes at work?"

Mike said, "No, it's been almost annoying with how things are running like clockwork since the dream."

"Well, you know, Mike, there are aliens out there, and the government works with them. I swear, something is fishy."

Mike and Joe gave Buzz that look of "Oh boy, here we go again."

"What's the weird suit guy been up to?" Buzz laughed.

"You mean Sebastian, Buzz."

"Yeah, right, Sebastian," Buzz answered in a mocking voice.

"Well, I haven't seen him lately. I know he is really under a lot of pressure to meet the deadline for the FDA approval meeting in two weeks. You know, Buzz, he's not so bad when you get to know him."

"Sure he's not, dresses like he thinks he's someone special, always talking on the phone. I got it. He's a G-man, yup, or a Russian spy. He's watching our every move," Buzz added.

Joe replied, "OK, well, I'm not sure he is anything but a typical businessman who is driven by money, so I guess that could be why he comes off as an entitled ass, but I highly doubt he's anything more than that, although he is intense." Joe continued. "Getting back to the valid point Buzz started with before he went all 'everyone is watching on us,' it had been about ten days since we've seen you. It is strange, Mike. Have you spoken to Stacy? Last time I talked to you, you said you were not feeling well and were heading home and then nothing. The restaurant said they got a text from you that you were ill and needed to meet the deadline on the project, so you wouldn't be in for the week. Not like that is out of the ordinary for you since you started with the whole—what is it again? Artificial rain?"

"That's another thing: who or what makes artificial rain? Not possible. I'm telling you, the government is out to get us. Mike, you're bringing bad mojo into the brewery, man, and it's starting to freak me out," Buzz said as he swiveled around, checking everyone's whereabouts in the brewery.

"Buzz, calm down, man. You don't have to be so paranoid all the time. You need to lay off the java." Joe laughed as Mike shook his head and agreed.

Mike raised his glass and said, "Now I would drink to that. You know, Buzz, lack of rain and droughts have affected not only the economy but also the quality of the food we are all eating, so yes, I felt very drawn to this project and do stand behind the theory. I sincerely hope we can figure it out. They have been working on the science behind it. My part is to make sure the quality and composition doesn't chemically alter the integrity of the food in both flavor and visible appearance. With all the GMO crap out there, we need an alternative for good, wholesome, healthy, organically grown produce that can withstand either the drought conditions or the ability to alter the drought conditions. Without Sebastian and his company, we wouldn't have the funding even to consider this. We need to be forward thinkers, Buzz. We're not in the '70s anymore."

"All right, Mike, let's not overwhelm poor old Buzz," Joe said as he handed Buzz a beer. "Here, old man, this one's on us!"

"Yes, Joe. To answer your question, I called Stacy earlier but apparently got a taste of my own medicine. It went to voice mail. Good for her. She must be taking that vacation she had been talking about for the last couple of months. She said they were planning to visit Georgia. I think they have family there or something."

CHAPTER SIX

J ESS HAD FINALLY settled into the guest room and decided to watch the nightly news. She reached for the volume as they were talking about the strange flu virus again; now the counts were up to forty-seven infected in Denver and thirteen confirmed cases that are being quarantined at Emory in Atlanta. The CDC plans on holding a news conference at 8:00 a.m. tomorrow. *Great, flu, perfect, just what we need*, Jess thought. Anya was sleeping soundly in her bed for the first time in a while. The stillness of the North Georgia night was peaceful.

The next morning, Anya was up early, making breakfast, when Jess smelled the bacon from upstairs. "Girl, that smells so good!" Jess yelled down to her. As she made her way to the kitchen, Jess told her how the smell of bacon and biscuits reminded her of when Sonya was still alive and would cook breakfast for them, especially the potato pancakes. "Anya, did your grandmother ever tell you some of the stories of Germany and the war? Or her time spent working there?"

"No, not really," she replied. "She said she was working on mostly agriculture projects and foodstuff, not very exciting according to her. She did share her childhood memories with me, though. She seemed to have had a happy life there. In fact, I think if she hadn't met my grandfather, she probably would have stayed there. I mean, her family remains there to this day. Her brother passed away, but she still has a sister, brother, nieces, and nephews all there. She would visit at least every other year. It's amazing how she stayed close with all of them, being so far away."

"So did you hear about the new flu virus?" Jess asked.

"Well, I heard something about it yesterday. Twenty cases in Denver or something like that, right?"

"I wonder if it will be like the stupid bird or swine flu. The media made it out to be so dangerous and, of course, caused hysteria. I heard last night on the eleven o'clock news there were more cases, and the CDC will hold a press conference today at eight."

"Well, put it on. It's just about eight now," Anya replied.

Jess reached for the remote and turned on the TV. The newscaster said, "Coming up after these messages, the live CDC press conference."

"Hey, it looks like it's coming on after the commercials," Jess said.

"OK, I'll bring in the plates. You grab the coffees." Sitting down on the couch side by side enjoying their breakfast, they waited for the press conference to start. "Turn it up. It's starting."

"Good morning, my name is Mrs. Hardy. I am the chief liaison officer for public relations for the CDC here in Atlanta. We have been closely monitoring this new strain of flu that is being seen both in Denver, Colorado, and here in Atlanta.

"First, I would like to go over the facts that we do know. Approximately three months ago, we started getting reports out of Denver that there were isolated breakouts of a new flu-like virus. At that time, it was isolated to one town and had not seemed to have spread. We had the local hospital report their findings to us. Out of the five people who originally contracted the virus, three passed away, one will require long-term medical care, and the other patient has recovered and does not seem to require additional treatment at this time.

"Since the first case of this virus, it appears to be spreading rapidly. With that being said, we do not want to cause any panic. We have established these safety guidelines as follows: Wash your hands after being in public areas, such as grocery stores, schools, and public buildings. If you have a cough or any flu-like symptoms, wear a mask and contact your health-care provider immediately. At this time, we are working closely with the top vaccine companies to try to develop a vaccine to combat this particular strain. Please keep in mind vaccine development does take several months to complete. At this time, we are still far away from a viable vaccine option.

"As of this morning, fifteen minutes before coming on the air, the new numbers for the outbreak are as follows: Denver has seen the brunt of this epidemic. There are over 579 infected at last count and 82 deaths. The local hospitals are working overtime to try to care for the growing numbers of sick. In Atlanta, we are now reporting a total of 235 confirmed cases and 58 deaths. The CDC is working with both state and local officials, as well as the hospitals in these areas. Here in Georgia, we are isolating all patients with confirmed cases to Emory. We will be making updates as needed on the status of both the vaccine and further instructions if plans change. Again, we do not want to cause panic at this time.

"Thank you for your time. I will take a few questions now. Yes, Fred, what's your question?"

"Thank you, Mrs. Hardy. You stated that, in the original outbreak, there was a need for long-term medical care. Could you elaborate on that?"

"I will be happy to give you the details I know. In that case, the patient exhibited both dementia-like symptoms and mild paralysis. It does seem to come and go, so we are closely monitoring that. OK, Marcy."

"Mrs. Hardy, do you have any data on how many patients are experiencing those symptoms you just mentioned?"

"I have limited info as of right now, but from preliminary reports, it appears to be as many as 70 percent." A gasp fell over the crowd. Now there were about twenty-five hands in the air to ask questions.

The physician who was standing next to Mrs. Hardy quickly stepped up to the podium in front of her, raised his hands, and said, "As Mrs. Hardy stated, there is a huge amount of data flooding us right now. We have teams going through all of it as we speak. It is just too early to speculate anything at this time. We will keep the public informed as we sift through the data. That will be all at this time. Sorry, but we need to get back to our work." He put his arm around Mrs. Hardy and escorted her out the door.

"Well, folks, you heard it here. Wash those hands, and I don't know about you, but I'm thinking of using those new services where you order your groceries online," the anchorman said to his weatherman and then turned it over to Jim for traffic.

"So it's a doozy this morning. Spaghetti Junction is quite the mess." You could hear in the background.

Anya looked at Jess and said, "Wow, this is almost unbelievable, and school is just getting under way for you, Jess."

"Yeah, it is. We always see a rise in the illness at the beginning of the year, but yikes, this does not sound good." Jess was an English teacher at the local high school. "Anya, don't you get updates from the CDC via e-mail from when you were a practice manager at the office?"

"Actually, you know what I'll do? Let me log on to that e-mail account and see if it has any info. So what do you have on your plate today, Jess?"

"Well, I have to run and get more school supplies. The budgets are getting smaller and smaller. Do you want to come with me?"

"I would, but I've got to get some of the last projects done around here. Call me later when you're done running around. And, Jess, thanks again for everything."

"Of course, no worries. Let me know if you need anything."

As Sebastian opened the door, he saw her standing there; it was Stacy. "I wasn't expecting you. Come in. Can I get you a drink, perhaps a brandy, to warm you up?"

"Sebastian, I am very sorry for bothering you at home, but I am concerned about Mike. He seems quite odd and almost delirious. He sent me an e-mail the day he didn't make it to the meeting, and it contained coordinates where to find him, a list of items to bring, and accurate instructions."

Sebastian walked over the antique desk in front of his father's portrait, sat in the large leather chair, and folded his hands in front of him on the desk. "Stacy, please join me. Take a seat, won't you?" Stacy walked over to the other side of the desk and sat facing him. "Please, Stacy, tell me your concerns. You have my undivided attention."

She started with Mike's behavior and then stated she also has been noticing some weird things with other team members that were making her uncomfortable. She said that there were invoices for supplies and random charges on the company credit card statement. "I spoke with

Bob in accounting, and he said it was above my pay grade and that I should not worry myself with things that don't concern me."

"Tell me, Stacy, did you notice anything else?" Sebastian calmly asked.

"Yes, sir, there were medical equipment, car rentals, nursing staff, bills paid to a physician, an invoice from a vaccine company. And that was just the tip of the iceberg." Stacy continued. "Mike wasn't feeling well, so when he was out, I went into his office, and there were notes scribbled on Post-its, but it was not his writing, sir. I've been working closely with Mike now, and I would recognize his writing anywhere. The notes had his address, a description of his car, the name of the diner and brewery where he hangs out. Sir, do you think someone is following him? Maybe because of the work we are doing with the project?

"I was still curious and, of course, did not want to bother you without getting cold, hard facts. I went to the security footage of the hall outside of the office and saw your driver entering and then exiting Mike's office the morning he disappeared, which I found a bit odd as we were all in the conference waiting for you. And the driver knows where to find you or Mike, so why would he be in there while everyone is in the meeting room? So I asked Jose, the security guard in the garage, if they had footage or a log of who had checked in that morning, but your driver wasn't signed in, and your car wasn't in the garage. Later that afternoon, Joe called the office looking for Mike. He said he had just disappeared from the diner in the middle of breakfast. Poof! He was gone. He did say he saw some weird tire tracks in the snow out back and that, from the looks of them, someone was in a hurry. That, of course, made me think, 'Odd tires, hmmm.' Just then, I remembered seeing an invoice about a month ago for your car. And well, I had never heard of those tires as they are custom to your imported car. Sir, I think your driver is maybe leaking info or, worse, behind Mike's disappearance.

"Then I receive the e-mail with the instructions. When I get to the location, I find Mike attached to all kinds of medical equipment, and a nurse tells me he was going to be OK, but they had to give him fluids. I'm so confused. Something is not right. I'm getting anxious about Mike. That night, when Mike woke up, I was going to tell him everything, but I didn't know where to start, and he seemed so sick. The next morning, he was gone."

"Is that everything, Stacy? I can see why you're concerned. I think it's time to take that vacation to Georgia to visit your family, lie low, and relax. I will handle this. And, Stacy, thank you so much for bringing this to my attention. In fact, let me make the travel arrangements for you. You deserve a break for all the hard work you have put in." Just then, Sebastian came around the desk and placed his hand on her shoulder. "How does that sound, Stacy? Why don't you bring your husband with you? You know, I just had a fantastic idea. Let's not tell your sister and make a surprise, shall we? Oh, how fun, Stacy! Who doesn't love a surprise?" Sebastian said.

He walked over to the shelf where there was a very ornately carved wooden box displayed. The inside of the box was lined with red velvet; in the middle was a small glass vial. The little bottle had a strange design on it and contained a cloudy-looking clear liquid. "Now, Stacy, how about that drink? We can drink to loyalty and surprises."

"OK, sir, that would be wonderful, and it would help calm my nerves a bit."

He proceeded to pour the contents of the vial into a glass and then added the liquor and stirred it. Walking toward Stacy and handing her a drink, he said, "Please call me Sebastian. After all, you have had my back with this big mess, and I appreciate it more than you'll ever know."

She reached for the glass as Sebastian said, "Here's to loyalty." And he raised his glass.

"Yes to loyalty," she replied and slowly drank the contents of the glass.

"Now, Stacy, with the weather so bad outside, I insist you let my other driver take you to the Westin at the airport. He has driven me since I was a young boy. I will have your car delivered to your home, and all your bags will meet you for your flight first thing in the morning. Let's call your husband and tell him the great news. Have him meet you at the Westin. Let him know you will be in the executive suite." He reached for her phone and handed it to her. "Go ahead, call him."

TRACY ANNE BERTINI

Stacy quickly dialed the number; her husband picked up on the first ring. "Hi, it's me," she said. "I have great news. Oh yes, it went well. Sebastian said he was very thankful for my loyalty." She looked over at Sebastian and smiled. "Well, guess what? We are going to Georgia! Sebastian has arranged everything. Isn't that amazing? We have been talking about it for years now. Oh, and the best part is it's a surprise. I know, won't they be tickled pink! All you have to do is meet me at the Westin Hotel. Yes, dear, the one at Denver International. He has arranged for us to stay in the executive suite, and our flight leaves first thing in the morning. We will be there for biscuits, gravy, and grits! I can't wait to see my sister's face." Stacy was over the moon; her husband had lost his job a year ago and had been looking for one this whole time. In the meantime, he had been doing odd jobs to help them stay afloat. "Oh yes, I love you too. I'll see you soon."

CHAPTER SEVEN

B UZZ WAS ALONE; he had just finished his nightly chores to close the brewery. He went upstairs and headed to bed. He reached out his hand and picked up the picture of Faith. "I love you, honey, still to this day. There isn't a day that goes by that I don't wish I could've taken your place. If only I didn't get drafted, I could have been here. I would have been driving. You'd still be with me."

He then opened the nightstand drawer and pulled out a photo of a sonogram; Faith had sent it to him in the mail while he was at war. It was a baby boy. "My son," Buzz said through tears. He grabbed the bottle of whiskey and drank till he passed out.

The next morning, he awoke with one heck of a headache. He heard his phone's message notification going off. "What the hell? Leave me alone." He reached for the phone and noticed five missed calls and ten new text messages. Most of them were from Pastor Thompson; Buzz had not returned his calls for some time now. Seeing the Thompsons reminded him of Faith, and that hurt too much.

I remember that day like it was yesterday. We were in a small village after winning the conflict. We had reestablished clean water and safety for the villagers. It was the only part of this war I could get behind. The poor, innocent people are suffering, women and children murdered senselessly. No one should ever feel unsafe in their home. That afternoon the mail came, he got a letter from Faith. He'd recognized her cute little swirls in her writing and how she always put a heart at the end of his name. He couldn't wait to read it. He went back to the tent, lay on his bunk, and opened the letter.

Dear Buzz,

I miss you more than words can say. I fondly think of the way you would play with my hair while we would lie for hours and talk about our future. I am counting the days till you come home. Only thirty more days, my love. Daddy and Mom send their love; mom is busy planning to have the whole town over for dinner when you get home. I hope you are ready. I am so proud of you and feel honored to become your wife in forty-five days; I'm counting the days, my love.

I have some fantastic news for you, Buzz: we are having a son. Open the little envelope I sent. It has our son's first photo. I wanted you to have it. Daddy and Mom both agreed to let our friends in on our secret; they said this baby is a blessing from God himself, and we don't get to pick the timing of such gifts. The ladies gave me a baby shower. Wait till you see all the baby stuff. It is everywhere.

Daddy finished the apartment for us over the garage; it is beautiful! Everyone from church pitched in; it's ready for you, complete with a sign that says, "Welcome to the Smiths." Mom and some of the ladies from church have been teaching me how to knit and, of course, to cook. I learned how to make your favorite meat loaf.

I was thinking about names. How do you feel about Isaiah or Matthew? I love both of those names.

I have all your clothes moved in, and your favorite chair is ready for you to catch the game with guys. It will be so perfect; it's everything we planned for and more. The baby is kicking all the time now. I wish you were here to feel it, but you'll be here for number two! Daddy talked to Mr. Richardson, and he said he would love to have you back at the garage when you get home.

Oh, and of course, a dollar more an hour. He told me you have extra mouths to feed. I have an appointment next week to check the baby's weight; I will write again after to give you an update.

You'll be here before we both can blink! You are my everything, and I will see you soon, my love. I am pretty tired. It's been hot here. Later I'm planning on taking the Corvette to get her shined up for you sometime over the next couple of weeks; she'll be all set for you. I can't wait to drive down the coast with you.

Good night, my love. See you in my dreams.

All my love,
Faith and Baby xoxo

A tear fell onto her signature, and Buzz wiped the other tears away. He placed the letter and photo back in the drawer. "I love you too, my love." He looked at his phone again and thought about calling Pastor; he started to dial.

Pastor Thompson answered, "Buzz, is that you, son?" Buzz was silent. "Son, I am here. Please talk to me. We love you." Buzz choked back his words, swallowed his tears, and hung up the phone.

He then got a new text: "Buzz, we love you. Thanks for letting us know you are OK. When you are ready, we are here—PT."

Pastor ran into the kitchen. "Cindy, he's OK! He just called."

Cindy spun around with tears in her eyes. "Oh, thank the good father above. What did he say?"

"He didn't," said Pastor. "But I heard him breathe, and he stayed on longer this time. I told him what we always tell him: we love him, and we are here for him when he is ready. Cindy, I feel it is our calling to keep reaching out to him. He is our boy. I pray for heavenly Father's guidance and to help him through his pain."

"Amen, I do as well. He wasn't the only one who lost the two of them."

"I know, Cindy, but he has fallen away from his faith in himself, our heavenly Father, and mankind. They were his world."

"I know. They were mine too." Tears began to run down her face as she excused herself to go to the bedroom. She grabbed her pillow and silently cried for the loss of her baby and her baby's baby. "Why did this happen to us?" She always put on a brave face and friendly smile in front of everyone else, but here, she could express her sorrow, pain, and emptiness in silence alone.

As Stacy's husband parked the car at the Westin, he happily grabbed the suitcases from the trunk and made his way to the doors. "Good evening, sir. Are you checking in?" the friendly voice said from the other side of the front desk.

"Why, yes, I am," he said cheerfully. "In fact, I'm meeting a beautiful woman in the executive suite, and then tomorrow we are flying to Georgia to spend time with family."

"Excellent, sir. I see your reservation right here. Oh, and it looks like everything has been taken care of. Wow, including dinner and complimentary couple's massage. Someone knows how to give the VIP treatment. Well, sir, I will have Josh bring up your bags, and I believe the young lady is already in the dining room waiting. Enjoy your stay. I'm Eric. If there is anything else I can do for you, please don't hesitate. Follow the marble floor to the dining room. She is seated near the window at the best table in the house."

"Thank you, Eric. I appreciate it." Walking through the door to the dining room, he noticed Stacy sitting exactly where he said she would be. He walked over and gave her a kiss on her forehead. "Hi, sweetheart. Did you order drinks yet?"

"No, I was waiting for you, hon," she replied.

The waiter came over and asked if they would like to order drinks and an appetizer yet. "Yes, we'd like to order a bottle of wine and will each have the house salad. Are you OK, sweetie? You look a little pale. Are you feeling ill?"

"I think I'm just tired. I just need some food and sleep. I'll be good and ready for our trip by the a.m. I'm sure of it," Stacy said.

"OK, let's get you some food then, and we can go upstairs, and I'll fill the bath for you."

"That sounds great. You always know just what I need. That's one of the reasons I love you so much."

Halfway through their dinner, Stacy sneezed and wiped her nose with the white napkin; when she looked at the cloth, there was blood on it. She looked at her husband, and before she could say a word, she had passed out on the floor and was bleeding from her nose.

"Quick! Someone call 911. My wife is ill!" he shouted as he placed his rolled-up jacket under her head. "Help, we need help now! Stacy, sweetie, please answer me, sweetheart, Stacy. Please help!" The tears ran down his face. "I don't think she's breathing. Will anybody help us? Why isn't the ambulance here yet? God, please, don't take her from me. Stacy!"

He laid his head on her chest to hear her last breath. "Dear God, *no*!" He held her lifeless body in his arms with his tear-soaked lips to her forehead. "No, no!"

"Sir, please step aside. We are here to help. Sir, please," repeated the paramedic.

"You're too late. She's gone. She's gone. Oh my god, she's gone."

CHAPTER EIGHT

A RRIVING EARLY TO the office, Mike went straight to the testing lab today. They have been working for weeks on the new test foods; he could not wait to see if their projections were closer this time. Sebastian had brought world-renowned scientists to help with this project. As Mike entered the lab, he noticed there was a bulb out in the greenhouse. "Oh great, we must have had another power surge. This won't work," he said out loud as he hastily walked into the greenhouse control room.

All right, which one was it? There were so many buttons and levers to pull, he thought. *Seriously, this can't be that hard.*

Just then, Kevin—his lab assistant and botanist—popped his head up from the last row of potatoes at the back of the greenhouse. "Hey, Mike, come on back. Boy, do I have something to show you!" There was so much excitement coming from his voice. He stood up and scrambled over to the table at the far end. "See? Look here, Mike, the potato we grew in the lab with AR-1 is actually better in color and texture, but that's not it." As he cut a slice of the potato, he pointed out, "Look at the color and texture. It's 100 percent even all the way through."

Mike quickly said, "OK, well, the suspense is killing me. Let's taste it. Remember, Kevin, the last three times we thought we had something, it usually failed because of human error. If we taste it and it is not pleasing, it's back to the drawing board with the potatoes."

"I know, Mike, but this looks like the best, freshest potato I've ever seen." Mike grabbed a chef's knife from the drawer. He sliced the potato up into quarters and quarters again.

"It is a smooth chop," Mike stated. "Let's boil a few. We will fry a few, and we will leave a few raw for testing purposes."

"Perfect! I'm in. Let's do it." Kevin threw his hand up, walked to the sink, and washed his hands. Mike grabbed two aprons from behind the door and gave one to Kevin. "Thanks, Mike." Kevin smiled and nodded. "Let's get busy up in here!" he said in an announcer-style voice.

Mike laughed and pointed toward the pot with now-boiling water. "Kevin, can you go ahead and add the potatoes to the water now. Please?"

"Chef, yes, Chef," Kevin replied. They plated up the different recipes, walked outside to their makeshift dining area, and sat down. "Here goes nothing." They both nodded and first took a bite of the fried option.

"It's delicious. The boiled one really did keep its shape and didn't crumble, and that's a plus for sure. I think we have finally perfected the ratio of artificial rain to organic compost fertilizer. I can't wait to test the other vegetables and fruits. We are going to have a long day, Kevin. Let's get to it!"

They proceeded to gather three to four samples per vegetable and fruit plants. After several hours, they were done with their testing, each tasting better than the last. "We've done it! It has taken three years, but we finally did do it. We can show now with cold, hard data that using the cloud-seeding method works and does not change the taste. In fact, we even feel it tastes better. Well, now we have to get the lab reports done to make sure the chemical composition is still the same. We have about one and a half weeks before we present to both the FDA for approval and the USDA for their endorsement. Once we have that in place, we will be traveling to the local farms and introduce it to them."

Anya decided to do some gardening that morning. As she walked through the roses, she realized some of the plants at the back of the house had been trampled. She walked closer and saw two footprints again—in fact, the exact same prints as in the front garden and the back door. *OK, someone was definitely watching me. Why?* she thought. She decided to go back to the library in Helen to research that strange brochure she and Jess found. *I can feel it in my gut it's all connected. I don't know how or why, but it is.*

Walking into the library, she headed right for the travel guide section. She pulled out a few books. She collected titles like *Secret Travel Getaways in Georgia*, *Monuments*, and *Off the Beaten Path*. These seemed like they would be a perfect place to start her research. Hours went by and still nothing. *I have to get to the bottom of this. I need a clue. Oh how I wish my grandmother were here.*

Just then, she looked up and saw the sun setting and shining right through the stained-glass window. *There it was, a sign—the stained glass. I need to find out somehow who designed the stained-glass windows in this area.* She checked a few titles about Georgia architecture and stained-glass artists.

Before I head home, I'll grab some dinner and pick up a thank-you gift for Jess. She loves jerky. The jerky snack shack store on River Street had the best jerky around. The owners were always so friendly that you could talk to them for hours. The owner Lawrence, took pride in the jerky that he made; he even had mastered a softer brisket jerky that Jess was obsessed with.

"Hello, Anya, what brings you into town today?" the shop owner asked.

"I had to go to the library to research a few things, and then I figured I had to come pick up some of that famous jerky," she said with a smile.

As they put together a package of their best flavor assortment, he asked, "So what are you researching?"

Anya replied, "Well, it's actually really hard to explain. Let's just say I'm starting with stained-glass window artists."

"I see. Well, you know if I can help you in any way, I'm here."

She closed her bag, put the jerky inside her purse, smiled, and said, "I know. Thank you."

As she left the store, she walked toward Main Street and the bridge when she happened to look up at another stained-glass window in the historic building right in front of her. *That sure looks like the same sand dollar in that stained-glass window.* She found it very strange that she had never noticed the similarity before with this window and the one at the cabin.

She walked up the old staircase and into the building. "Hello, is anyone here?" She raised her voice a bit. "Hello? I'm sorry to bother you. I just have a quick question about your window. Hello?" *I'll go eat dinner and try to stop back on my way back to the jeep*, she thought.

Sitting on the banks of the Chattahoochee River, she enjoyed her knockwurst with sauerkraut, German potato salad, and red cabbage; and of course, it was served with a piece of fresh rye bread, just like how Sonya would eat. The cool breeze came off the water while a few late tubers went down on their inflatable tubes. She had many fond memories of riding the Hooch in a tube during the summers at the cabin.

As she paid the check, out of the corner of her eye, she noticed a strange man sitting on the far side of the tavern. It was weird because no one would ever wear an all-black wool suit in the Georgia heat. As they made eye contact, he quickly folded his newspaper and placed it on his lap to conceal something that looked like a gun. He stood up and hastily left the restaurant while almost knocking over the waitress on his way out. He ran up the stairs onto the bridge, and he was gone.

Anya motioned to the waiter. "Did you see that man? Has he been here before? Do you know why he was in such a hurry?"

The waiter said, "Actually, come to think of it, I've never seen him in here before. He was very short with me and demanding to sit at that table as it is slightly concealed by the foliage of the tree. Why? Is everything OK, ma'am?" She stared up the staircase for a few moments, still feeling her heartbeat in her chest pounding harder and harder. "Ma'am, are you all right?" The waiter repeated himself.

She shook her head and said, "Oh, I'm sorry. I, umm, yes . . . I, ah . . . I'm OK. That man looked like he was concealing a—well, you know what? Just forget it. I'm sorry I bothered you." She collected her belongings and decided to head up the staircase.

"Thank you. Have a nice evening, ma'am!" the waiter yelled as she swiftly ran up the stairs to the main road and looked all around; there was no sight of him.

Who was he, and what does he want? She began to let her imagination get the best of her again. *This had to be the man who ransacked my house.*

Anya headed back to the building with the stained-glass window. *I sure hope someone is there now.* She opened the door and walked back inside. "Hello, is there anyone here? I just have a couple of questions, if you don't mind."

After a few minutes, an elderly woman came walking out from a back room. "I thought I heard someone. What can I do for you, young lady?" she asked.

"My name is Anya. I was wondering if you had information about the artist who may have made the stained-glass window."

"Oh, that window has been here since 1915. In fact, I believe it was brought over from Germany around that time."

"So you have no idea who made it?" Anya asked.

"Well, if my memory serves me right, I do recall a man named— well, now what was his name? He was a handsome man, dressed really well. It was a kind of strange name."

"So this was the artist?" Anya asked again.

"Oh, no, honey, I have no idea who made it, but there was a man a few years ago, four or five years ago, in here asking the same sort of questions. I couldn't help him, which seemed to really infuriate him. He actually left and slammed the door behind him, mumbling under his breath. You know, we see all types up here. Everyone loves to visit and vacation here." She continued. "There's not too many of us who are originals. Oh, where are my manners? My name is Millie, and you said your name was Anya. Is that right?"

"Yes, it is. It's very nice to make your acquaintance, Millie. How long have you owned this building?"

"Well, my daddy actually bought it back in the twenties. You know, Helen officially became a city in 1913. It is actually the sister city of Füssen, Bavaria, FRD. Not that you asked me but it is a pretty neat little bit of trivia about our city. So I do know there was an original owner who had the stained-glass window put in, but it was here when Daddy bought the building."

"Is there any way we can go upstairs and look at it closer?" Anya hoped her new friend, Millie, would allow her to.

"Well, sweetheart, you can. These hips do not permit me to go up and down those stairs anymore, but please go ahead straight through the hall, and you'll see the staircase, and it's on the second-floor landing."

"Oh thank you, Millie. I won't be long. Thank you again." She quickly made her way down the hall and up the stairs. *There it is, even more beautiful in person*, she thought. Standing there, she was taking in all the fine details of the window—the heavy leading and intricate patterns that reminded her of vines. In the center of the window, just like the one in the cabin, was a sand dollar. She took out her phone and proceeded to take a few photos up close of each section and a few of the full window. It was absolutely beautiful.

After spending a while on the landing, she noticed something again on the side of the sand dollar; there was something written. *Maybe this was just the artist's way of signing his pieces.* Unlike the one in the cabin, this one had the number 111 and no apparent letters. She took a close-up of the numbers to study when she got home. She could then compare them to hers.

Almost running down the stairs, she just about knocked Millie over as she headed to the door. "Oh thank you again, Millie. I think I've found exactly what I'm looking for. If you can remember anything else about the window, the building, the area, or anything at all, please call me."Anya handed Millie a Post-it where she had scribbled her phone number on for her.

"Of course, will do, although I am getting up there in age, you know. It was a pleasure to meet you, and I'm sure I will see again soon."

"Bye, Millie!" Anya yelled as she ran out the door.

She immediately decided to head back to the library. *Had I missed a sand dollar in that stained-glass window? I really don't recall one being there*, Anya thought. She walked back into the library and rushed over to the window, but there was no sand dollar design, no intricate vines—actually, no clue that the same artist even did this one. *Hmm, I better get home and take a look.*

She jumped into the jeep and headed back down the alternate Route 75 toward her peaceful valley on the side of the mountain where the mountains met. The sun was just starting to set. *Good, I'll still have time*

TRACY ANNE BERTINI

to see the window, she thought as she drove down the driveway and put the jeep in park outside of the cabin. She reached for her keys, unlocked the front door, and stepped inside. She was in a hurry; as she threw her purse on the kitchen table, it missed the corner and spilled everything on the floor. *Well, I will have to get back to that. I'm losing daylight.*

She walked down the hall to the staircase. There it was, her window. Taking out her phone, she studied both windows and noticed they were virtually the same window except it looked to be a mirror image of each other. *OK, what is the connection? Come on, Anya, think.* She held her hands to the side of her forehand and rubbed her temples. *What is the connection?* Then she thought, *What is 333 and 111? They are clearly not the same number, so what could be the similarity? Could it be the number of each design, like mine was number 333, and the other was 111?* It could be plausible, but in her gut, she knew it was not the case. There was something much bigger going on here behind these windows.

She dialed Jess's cell. "Hey, Jess, it's me. How was school today? That's great news. I'm glad you got that promotion. The degree paid off! We will have to celebrate soon. Oh yeah, right. I called, well, to say hi and to tell you I found another stained-glass window in Helen. It could be my window's twin. Well, no, not twin. It's a mirrored image and has a different set of numbers. I know, I have no idea. Well, I spoke with a woman named Millie. Her father has owned it since the twenties. No, it's OK. Yes, call me in the morning. I'm going to relax and see if I can find anything else out. My grandmother has some old photo albums around here somewhere. I'll see you tomorrow then. OK, bye." Anya hung up the phone.

She opened the hall closet. *Now where the heck are those photos? Ugh, what a mess!* She had not been in that closet past where she kept her yoga mat. It was a large closet; she used to play hide-and-seek in it as a child. She would hide for hours, pretending it was her castle.

Anya did not know her father; he left when she was only one and a half years old. He was married, but her mother had no idea. She often tried to find him but was always met with disappointment. She always would wonder, *Do I look like him? Do I have more family?* She always felt like something was missing deep down inside as if she didn't truly know

, where she came from or who she was. She had always hoped someday she would find him or her family. Growing up without her family was isolating; they had to be out there somewhere. Did they ever wonder about her? Did they even know she existed?

Her mother always worked hard to provide for her children. Anya's mother was a free spirit and loved to travel, especially to the deserts of Arizona. That was her happy place. She hadn't made it to Georgia in a few months as she was caring for Anya's ill sister.

Anya's sister had seven children and was always busy shuttling someone here or there. Over the last few years, she had been fighting a mysterious illness. The top doctors in Boston were stumped. What did she have? As she grew weaker, their mother helped nurse her to health. Anya could not stand being so far away and would often feel helpless. The sisters would talk on the way to work; they both enjoyed their phone calls to catch up with each other.

CHAPTER NINE

O NE NIGHT, WHEN Johnathon's secret society was meeting at the house, Sebastian decided he would hide in the library before the men would enter. Hopefully, he would finally see and hear what the masters of the universe would do for hours in the wee hours of the morning. He told his father he was feeling ill and was heading to bed early; of course, his father's response was more of the same. "Of course, you worthless sick child, you wrecked the whole plan. The thought of him having my last name is embarrassing! Ms. Charlotte, get him out of here. His face disgusts me!"

Sebastian held back tears as he took her hand. "I don't need you to tuck me in, Ms. Charlotte. I'll be OK. Good night. I'll see you at breakfast," he said as he turned and walked up the stairs toward the east wing.

Ms. Charlotte loved Sebastian, and it hurt her to see how Johnathon treated his son. *How can he be so vile?* She often thought of stealing Sebastian and taking him back home to South Carolina with her.

As Ms. Charlotte walked back toward her room, Sebastian sneaked down the back staircase, knowing he had about ten minutes to get to the library and hide without being noticed. His father had gone up to his room to put on his sacred robes. The robes they wore were long, black, and hooded. They reminded Sebastian of monk's robes. They also wore large pendants that hung to their midchest; each also had a ring on their right ring finger with a large stone in it. He noticed that, when the men got here, they were always dressed in all black from head to toe; and then as the ritual would begin, they would each pull out their robe and jewelry and begin to chant in unison. This seemed to take approximately thirty minutes from the beginning of the ritual; it reminded Sebastian of when he would attend church with his mother as a young boy.

He heard someone coming, so he climbed into the bottom of the liquor cabinet; there was a small door on the right, and it was a perfect hiding place to hear and see everything through its grated mesh. Just as he shut the door quietly, the men started to enter the library one at a time in single file; they each stopped at a statue and kissed its forehead and bowed. Then one by one, they would make their way to the long tables and begin the robing ritual. This seemed to go on for another thirty minutes; he noticed they had not stopped chanting through this whole process. *What were they saying?* he thought. He didn't recognize the language; he assumed it may be Latin or Greek.

He continued to watch as two men proceeded to chant individually as they lit the candles; it must have been over one hundred of them once they were all lit. All the men then knelt and bowed as a man began to place his hand on each of their heads and chant over them. After this part of the ritual was done, they stood up and, again in a single line, walked straight toward the bookcases at the far end of the library, each holding a single white candle.

He could not believe his eyes when he saw what happened next. His father placed his hand on a light fixture and turned it clockwise at about three on a clock. He heard a rumble, and then just like magic, the bookcase opened and revealed a stone passageway lit by candles; the men all entered and headed down the stone staircase. *Where are they going? How will I know what they are doing?* he thought. But he was much too afraid to come out of his hiding place yet. Sebastian stayed put, and when he finally thought the coast was clear, he followed them.

The hospital was overcrowded the night they brought Stacy's body in. Her husband had stayed by her side the whole time. He was shaken; he just witnessed the love of his life take her last breath. Jeff was all alone now. He heard his phone ringing from his pants pocket; he answered, "Hello?"

On the other end of the phone was Stacy's father, Chris. Through the tears, he replied, "Yes, sir, and she is gone. I don't even know how to explain it." He continued. "Yes, I agree she should be buried in Georgia with her mother. I will make the arrangements tomorrow. I need to take a bit just to figure this all out. I'll call you in the morning." He ended the call.

Sitting in the trauma bay at the hospital, all the activities in this room had ceased. He couldn't help but notice how quiet and alone it had become. How did this happen? They were about to share a wonderful vacation with family, exactly what Stacy and Jeff needed. *Now she is gone, just gone.* He sat in silence staring at the wall, still grasping Stacy's cold, lifeless hand. "What am I going to do without you? I can't bear to never hear your voice again or see that smile, which just lights up the room." Jeff was speaking to her as if she were just resting. "I love you so much. I can't go on without you. Stacy, why did you leave me here alone? We were supposed to grow old together, have children and grandchildren. The pain is too much to bear. I just want to die and be with you wherever you are."

Since being out of work, Stacy had taken on the breadwinner role in their relationship. She didn't complain, just did what she had to do and jumped right in. Jeff adored her very much. She was so caring, definitely inquisitive, and the most hardworking woman he had ever met. Last year, they let her life insurance policy lapse just to make the house payment. He couldn't tell her father; he would figure it out. *How much does it even cost to transport her back to Georgia? Oh, and then all the actual funeral expenses, I'm sure that is expensive.* He placed his hands over his eyes and broke down.

Just then, a dark shadow stood in the doorway and softly said, "Excuse me, but may I come in? I do not mean to intrude." Jeff took a moment to gather himself and wipe away the tears from his face. He looked up, wiped his eyes, and tried to adjust his sight to the low lighting in the room. Standing behind the man was a nurse and another man in a suit.

"I just want to be left alone, if you'll excuse me," Jeff said to the group standing in the doorway.

"If I may, I don't believe we have been formally introduced, although I feel like I know so much about you, Jeff, if I may call you that." The man started to walk into the light, his hand extended. "Let me introduce myself. My name is Sebastian. I knew Stacy very well. I am truly sorry for your loss. Stacy was a wonderful soul. She will be missed by many. I'm sure the timing isn't great. However, I would like to offer my assistance with her memorial and funeral expenses. I have arranged the travel back to Georgia already for you to take her home. Please allow me to do this for you to honor her."

Jeff welled up with tears again. "I am shocked. I do not even know how to reply to that," he said. He reached for Sebastian's hand and firmly shook his hand. "Sebastian, you worked so closely with her, often spending more time with her than me. She would want you there. I will only accept your offer if you are there."

"Of course, I wouldn't be anywhere else. Let me drive you home, and I will arrange a car for you tomorrow. We will go through the flower choices and details together. We will be departing for Georgia at 1:33 p.m. on my private jet. I have a nurse and my attorney with me. They will take care of escorting Stacy to my plane in time for departure tomorrow."

"Stacy was right. You are, at the very least, thorough. I would like to thank—"

Sebastian stopped him midsentence. "There is no need. I am here to help. When you are ready, we will take you home. If you would allow the nurse to come in, she will get Stacy cleaned up and escort her to a private room for the night, where I have arranged my personal medical team to do all necessary preparations and any tests you may want to be run. The results will be stat ordered, of course, directly to you."

"It appears you have taken care of everything. I don't even know what the standard tests to run are," Jeff said.

The nurse stepped out from the shadow of the doorway. "We would run a chem panel, as well as toxicology screening, a basic test like that."

"OK, that sounds reasonable. Would we find out what caused . . ." He paused, took a deep breath to compose himself again, and continued. "Her death?" He turned toward the nurse as he finished his question.

"Yes, sir. In combination with the medical examiner's exam and report, this is how we determine the cause of death."

TRACY ANNE BERTINI

"OK, may I have a moment to say goodbye?" They left the room, leaving Jeff and Stacy alone. He bent over, kissed her, and said, "I'll always love you." He followed Sebastian out of the hospital.

The car pulled into the driveway, and the driver stepped out and pulled open the door on Jeff's side of the car. "Sir, we have arrived at your residence."

Sebastian extended his hand once again and expressed his condolences and added, "I will you see you tomorrow. Is there anything else that you need tonight?"

Leaving the car, Jeff shook his head and said, "No, but thank you. You have already done so much for Stacy. I have no idea how to repay your kindness."

"No need," said Sebastian. The driver closed the door, and Jeff walked up his front stairs into the house as Sebastian watched from the back seat of the sedan.

CHAPTER TEN

"WE APOLOGIZE, BUT we are interrupting the regularly scheduled broadcasting to provide this exclusive update from the CDC. Overnight, the cases of the infected have exploded. We are now seeing cases in half of the country. The death toll has risen to over 2,901 in the United States alone. We are going live now to Sophia, who has been at the CDC headquarters all night with this developing story. Sophia, can you tell us what has happened? Do they have any idea why this is spreading so rapidly?"

"Bill, they have no idea. Everyone is frantically trying to find a trend in the data. They are saying this flu is nothing like they have ever seen. They have started to set up quarantine locations. If anyone has symptoms, they are asking you to now home-quarantine and call the CDC. They will then send a team to you and determine whether or not you will need to go to the CDC quarantine location. I have spoken with Ms. Hardy several times over the last twenty-four hours. She is working extremely hard as is everyone here.

"Here are the facts we know so far on the developments over the last twenty-four hours. The virus has definitely spread with record numbers of infected across the country. We have not seen anything like this in our history. The CDC spokesperson has been in contact with France, England, Germany, and Italy. We haven't received confirmation of reports stating they have seen the same illness. Although there have been unconfirmed reports of as many as 29,876 possible infected people in those countries. Bill, it looks like Ms. Hardy will need a few more moments before she steps to the podium. Like I was saying, it does appear as if the flu-like virus had now spread to Europe.

"I spoke with a young woman who is attending Georgia Tech just a few moments ago, and she told me the campus clinic has been packed with sick students, as well as faculty. In fact, they are saying they may cancel classes if the illness continues to spread at this pace. Oh, Bill, Ms. Hardy is approaching now. I'm going to turn it over to her."

"Good afternoon, ladies and gentlemen. Again, for those of you who do not already know, my name is Ms. Hardy. I am in charge of public relations for the Atlanta office of the CDC. As most of you have heard, we are dealing with a very contagious virus that is now spreading rapidly not only across this country but now, as confirmed, in the major cities in Europe as well. We are sorting through the data as quickly as we can. We have assigned multiple teams running twenty-four-hour shifts until we can find some information that could be useful to aid us in our fight against this deadly virus. Since yesterday, we have seen the virus spread at an alarming rate.

"We are now asking citizens to shelter in place. The state has declared a state of emergency in both Denver and Atlanta. All noncritical employees will be sent home and asked to remain there until we can get a handle on the situation. We have suspended flight service between Denver and Atlanta. To any travelers who have been stranded in either area, we will escort you to a designated quarantine area. And if you remain symptom-free for seven days, you will be allowed to take a bus to your destination. We are sorry for any inconvenience this will cause, but we are confident these safeguards will help slow the spread of the virus down."

Anya stood in the doorway and listened to the remainder of the news conference. *How could this be happening?* she thought. She walked over to the kitchen table and started to sift through her piles of books and information she checked out of the library. *Where do I start? It's going to be a long afternoon. It was about three o'clock now. I'll make one more cup of coffee.* She walked over to the cappuccino machine, grabbed her mug, and made a cup. As she took a sip of the warm coffee, she made her way back over to the table, sat down, and started looking at everything.

She studied the brochure with the faded pillars. *Why was this here? What was it?* She looked over her photos on her phone at the other stained-glass window. *What did the number 111 stand for?* She grabbed her cell and walked over to the window in the cabin. *Number 333,* she thought. *Hmm, 333.* She noticed on her phone it was now 3:20 p.m. *Wait, do you think it could be the time 3:33 p.m.?*

She held the photo up to the window; the numbers 111 and 333 were in the same spot but in a mirrored view. Just then, she started to feel the warmth on her feet from the sun that shone through the window; she always loved that feeling. She looked down at the floor and noticed the perfect sand dollar now being illuminated on the wood floorboards. Looking up toward the window again, she noticed the clock said 3:32 p.m.

She looked back down at the floor and noticed something very odd: one of the spines on the sand dollar was exactly over the seam in the flooring. As the clock turned 3:33 p.m., she saw something shiny in between the wood floorboards. *What was that?* She knelt down and ran her finger over the boards. It felt slightly raised. She tried to put her nail under and lift it, but it was too heavy. *I need to go get something to lift the floorboard.*

She quickly walked out to the garage and dug through the toolbox on the workbench. *Aha, this will work.* She picked up a small putty knife and headed back inside the cabin. Anya went to work with the putty knife, trying to pry up the floorboard. She slid the thin metal end of the tool under the edge of the board and gently pulled up.

There was quite a bit of space in the secret compartment. She reached her arm inside, and she was now shoulder deep. Anya pulled out her arm, and in her hand was an old leather-covered book, a key ring with four keys on it, a large folded map, and a handgun. *What was all of this? Who put it there?* She gathered the items and brought them over to her table to add to the already cluttered pile.

She sat back down and carefully picked up the book; it was beautiful. She wiped away the dust and saw the letters SGD on the cover. There it was again, the same letters that were in the stained glass, and they were also her grandmother's initials. She didn't recognize the book. Carefully holding the cover, she opened the book, and she noticed the edge of each page was gold. It was a very well-made book; the front had a sand dollar on it, just like the windows. It was raised and also made of leather as if it were carved into the cover. She turned it over and noticed some other ornate designs. She gently slid off the ribbon that was holding the book closed. The pages were yellowed and delicate. The first page had a handwritten note:

To my dear Anya,

The fact that you've found my book is a true testament to your persistence and inability to give up. What you are about to be a part of is so much bigger than all of us. You will need to push through even when you think you can't. Remember our time together; it will point you in the right direction and give you the tools you are going to need. I wish I could've told you everything when I was still there, but the timing wasn't right. I have tried to leave little hints that you would find to help, but I did not want anyone else to be able to figure it out. You are so much closer than you think to all the answers you've always searched for. Be patient. All will reveal itself in due time. This book was my life's work. Keep it safe. Always remember to be true to yourself and embrace life. It is a real gift. Watch your back as you get closer to the truth; it will become difficult to not draw attention to yourself. There is a whole network of people that have made its life purpose to see this plan fulfilled. We must not let it happen. Events have already been put in motion decades ago, but the timing was not right. I have put people in place to help guide you and protect you on this journey. The fate of life as we know it is in your hands!

Love,
Omi

Anya sat for a few minutes just staring at her grandmother's writing; it had been a few years since she had seen it. It brought back so many emotions: happiness as she felt her presence with her for a moment, sadness at the loss of her, and confusion about what was going on. She continued to look through the first few pages; they mostly consisted of math equations and what looked like lab reports. On the third page, she noticed it was titled "AR." She began reading. *What is AR?* she thought. She read the following:

> By combining silver iodide, potassium iodide, and dry ice (solid carbon dioxide). Liquid propane, which can be expanded into a gas, can also be used. The liquid propane can produce ice crystals at higher temperatures than the silver iodide. Next several rounds, we plan on using table salt (as it is hygroscopic) to study results. We should be able to increase the snowfall amounts produced by the clouds if the temperatures are between 19°F and -4°F (-7°C and -20°C). Introducing a substance such as silver iodide, which has a crystalline structure similar to ice, should induce freezing nucleation.

She paused for a moment and reread it. *I have no idea what this is and what it all means,* Anya thought. Her grandmother was working on artificial rain. Sonya did tell her she worked with agriculture in Germany, but she had no idea this was what she was working on. *I wonder why she never mentioned it to me.* Knowing her the way Anya did, her grandmother would've been proud of her work. It seemed strange to have never heard anything about it.

Suddenly, there was a loud knock on the front door. She jumped as it caught her off guard. She placed the book under the newspaper on the table and put a couple of magazines over the piles of things she was sifting through for research. Walking over to the door, she looked out the window to see who was out there on the porch. It was two men and a woman dressed in black suits. They looked official. "I'm not interested," she said through the door. She figured they were local members of a

TRACY ANNE BERTINI

church trying to spread the Word and invite her to their church. This often happened even way out here. They were still standing there, so she opened the door just enough to say "no, thank you."

The larger gentleman quickly introduced himself. "Ma'am, good afternoon. Please allow me to introduce myself. My name is Jeremy and we—"

She interrupted him as politely as she could, "Jeremy, it is nice to meet you, but I am extremely busy, and I'm not interested. I am already a member of a local church, but do have a good day." She started to close the door, and she looked down; just then, she got an uneasy feeling in her gut. She noticed his shoes; though they were shined and obviously expensive, they had red clay around the edges. It was apparent he had been off a walkway, say, walking in a rose garden. *Could this be the man who had broken in?* She quietly pushed her foot against the back of the door and continued to tell the group she was not interested.

The woman stared at her, put her arm in front of Jeremy, and said, "Oh, dear, do forgive us. We will be going. Sorry to have bothered you." Jeremy turned toward her and started to back away from the door. The strange woman continued. "We are new to the area and was just out trying to introduce ourselves to our neighbors. You see, we bought the old Jackson farm just down the road. Please accept our humblest apologies. Come on, let's be on our way."

They turned and started down the walkway when the woman turned around and said eerily, "We will see you soon. Good luck on your research." Anya quickly closed the door and spun around, looking at the table; there was no way she could've known she was researching anything. She locked the door and rushed over to the French doors and made sure those were locked as well.

When Anya picked the book back up, a loose paper fell out of it. The paper had an address on it. She quickly googled the address; it was in Denver.

CHAPTER ELEVEN

B UZZ ANSWERED HIS phone. "Hey, Joe, what's up?"
"Has Mike come by yet, Buzz?"
"Nah, I haven't seen him. Everything OK?"
"Did you hear about Stacy?"
"No, what about her?" Buzz asked.

"She passed away last night. She was eating at the Westin with Jeff and passed out after getting bloody nose or something, but that was it. I talked to Jeff for just a few minutes this morning. He is flying back to Georgia today to bring her back home and have her buried next to her mother. Can you watch over the diner for me? I'll only be gone for three days. The staff has it under control. They'll only call if they really need something. I appreciate it, Buzz."

"No problem, Joe. I am sorry for your loss. I know how close you, Jeff, and Stacy have gotten over the last three years. She was genuinely a nice person. She will be missed," he said.

"Thanks again, man. I wish it were a better reason to take me back to Georgia."

"All right, safe travels, Joe." Joe hung up the phone, finished packing, and headed to the airport. As he drove, he called Mike.

"Hey, man what's going on?" Mike asked.

"I am heading to the airport now. What time is your flight?"

"The private jet leaves at 1:33 p.m. I'm walking to the terminal now. When does yours leave, Joe?"

"My flight is at three. I have to make a stop on the way to the airport."

"I'll see you in Georgia, buddy. Safe travels."

"You too, Mike." Joe entered the freeway and headed south toward Denver International Airport. He had mixed emotions about heading to Georgia; he had lived there for years. He started thinking about his life in Georgia, and his wife—oh how he adored her; they were best friends. He still remembered the day she walked into his high school, and he approached her and gave her a hard time, saying, "Oh, I know you. You're football guy's girl."

She replied quickly and did not miss a beat. "OK, well, I'm no one's girl. So you are wrong, but you usually are," she said with a smile and walked past him. He loved her sassy attitude; it made him laugh.

They had met the year before when they both ran track for their high schools in Massachusetts. They would pass the hours debating how men were better than women and vice versa. He loved the fact she played hard to get; he accepted the challenge. He would walk the same way she did after school; he always played the same game. "So where are you going, Palsy?" he would ask only to get under her skin.

She would reply, "The same place I went yesterday. Oh! And the day before." She would laugh. "Work, you know, where you go to make money instead of always asking for it at the lunch table."

He said, "Well, I have a job too, you know."

"OK, I'll bite," she said. "Where do you work?"

"The same place you do." He laughed.

"Nope, you definitely don't work at the catering company. I think I'd know that," she replied. They continued their playful banter as they turned the corner to walk up the driveway to the caterers.

He walked in front of her and through the door and said, "So I need a job. Are you guys hiring?"

The man in the office replied, "Sure, we could use an extra set of hands around here."

Joe turned around and said, "See? I work here too!" He was quite proud of himself at this point.

She shook her head, walked by him, grabbed her apron, and started her tasks she had to get done for the wedding this weekend. "Well, I guess if you work here, then get to work. You can prep the salads," she said.

Their playful relationship had continued to grow over the next couple of weeks; he would lock her in the freezer for just a few seconds and then rescue her. Of course, she would always say, "You know I didn't need your help. I so could've gotten out myself. I don't need a man. I may want one but definitely don't need one!" There was that spunk again that he found so attractive. She was so independent and strong. He was always impressed with her. She always stayed positive and would figure out a way to get through whatever was thrown her way. She would often catch him looking at her from across the kitchen at work, and of course, when their eyes would meet, he would look away.

She always knew he was kind and had a big heart. Last year at the junior prom, she had gone with her ex-boyfriend, who was cheating on her, but she did not know. Joe came over to her as she sat at the table and started talking to her, making her laugh so she would not see the two of them dancing together. He was that kind of guy. Humor was his gift to the world.

On Friday, he called her and asked what her plans were. She replied, "Heading to the football game and pizza, Why? What are you doing tonight?"

"Wow, what a coincidence! So am I. Well, maybe I'll see you there," he said. He had already arranged for her friend to ditch her so she wouldn't have a ride home.

About seven minutes into the last quarter of the game, he made his move. "So hey, there you are. I haven't seen you all night," he said with a smile.

"I can't find them anywhere. We were going to leave about now to head to Brother's to get pizza," she replied.

"I actually just saw them pull out when I was coming back in."

"Great, that was my ride!"

"No worries, I've got you," he said. "Come on, the game is a blowout anyway. I'm hungry. Let's go get pizza." They decided to leave and head to the pizza place. Joe's favorite food was pizza hands down. They talked for hours that night about everything; it seemed like it was just the two of them in the whole world and time stood still. From that point on,

TRACY ANNE BERTINI

they were two peas in a pod. Although they had hiccups along the way, their friendship was the glue that held them together in tough times.

The small apartment on Wilder Street had become the home they built for each other. Although they missed Stoneham, Lowell was definitely more affordable, and they lived at the top of her grandparent's street. They had many great memories on Canton Street on the front porch while talking, playing card games, and of course eating pizza.

Their first Christmas in their own home was one of the most memorable for them both. Always wanting to play Santa to everyone else, she took the money out of their joint checking account to make sure to have gifts for everyone else. Joe arrived home from work that night and questioned her about the lack of money in the account; she confessed and started to debate her cause just like a professional attorney would have. Joe listened to her, the whole time falling in love with her all over again; she was a kind soul with the biggest of heart. This was another reason he could not live without her. He told her that it was OK, and he understood.

They went to her grandparents' house every Christmas Eve. In fact, this had been a family tradition for not only family but friends as well. There was music and so much food. Hundreds of Christmas cookies were baked and handed out as gifts. Her family was very musical and would sing and play instruments. The highlight of the evening would be the singing of "The Twelve Days of Christmas." Each person had a part; of course, she was "five golden rings." The house smelled like warm punch and cookies; it felt like home.

This year was special, though. Joe sat and watched her with her family. He thought. *She is so beautiful inside and out.* His best friend was always there to give him a pep talk or encourage his dreams, and his heart was full. The night ended, and they said their goodbyes and started on the very short walk home. The snow had begun about an hour before.

"Christmas snow," she said with a childlike smile. "You know, it is magical." She had a smile from ear to ear.

Joe often thought of this moment; in fact, he would've kept it frozen in time if he could have. "Let's go home, my lady." They finished their walk as she caught snowflakes on her tongue. They stood on the front step to the apartment building. He put his hand on the door so she could not go in, grabbed her tight, and held her, whispering in her ear, "You know I love you, right?"

She smiled and said, "Yes, I love you too."

The stars and moon were shining as the beautiful white snow fell almost silently on the ground. They stood there for a few more moments, and he kissed her on the forehead and said, "Oh, you're cold baby. Let's go in. Merry Christmas, sweetheart I love you."

The next morning was quiet; they cuddled and cooked breakfast together, listening to music and making pancakes. They were still waiting for their furniture to be delivered, but because of the holiday, it wouldn't be here until after New Year's. Again, they made do with what they had. They threw a mattress on the floor, lit candles, and had picnics often in the living room.

Her grandmother insisted that every house must have a Christmas tree, so she had given them her old tree with all the red and gold trimmings for it. They sat and watched the twinkling lights together as they ate their pancakes. Joe turned to her and said, "Well, do you want to get dressed?"

"No, I think I'll stay in my pj's. It's still snowing, and we aren't going anywhere, so why bother?"

They spent the day together sitting in front of the lit tree and talking for hours. He loved listening to her voice. Later that day, there was a knock at the door; it was her grandmother with a veggie tray, a box of doughnuts, and a sparkling cider. "Grammy, what are you doing?" She laughed.

"My, honey, aren't you going to get dressed?" she replied. Joe just stood and watched. He took the food from Grammy and placed it on the counter.

Soon after that, there was another knock; this time, it was her mother and sister. "Aren't you going to get dressed?" they asked.

They were all standing in the kitchen when there were two more knocks; this time, Joe's aunt and sister entered. Everyone was standing

TRACY ANNE BERTINI

and talking; this was the type of families they both had, showing up unannounced with food in hand.

On the next knock, Joe asked her to answer the door. There in the doorway was a man dressed in a black suit with a minister collar. Joe opened the door wider and said, "Please come in."

Joe stood and grabbed her hands and said, "Well, you left me no money to buy you a gift for Christmas, so all I have to give you is me. Will you marry me? Right here, right now, in front of our friends and family?" He pulled out a small box that had two gold bands. "OK, so we will get better ones someday. What do you say, love?"

She looked at him, smiled, and then said, "What? I can't get married in my pajamas! Wait, I have to find something to wear!" She rushed to the closet and grabbed a dress she would often wear for church. "No time to do my hair." She pulled out her big black hat and threw it on. It wasn't what she would've chosen to wear for her wedding, but she was marrying her best friend.

Joe walked through the bedroom door and asked her if she was OK with getting married this way. He added, "One day we can renew our vows and have the wedding of your dreams, I promise."

She hugged him and said, "As long as you're here, let's do it." As the few family and friends gathered in the living room of the small apartment on Wilder Street, they exchanged their vows in front of the lit Christmas tree in a small but very meaningful ceremony. They had finally tied the knot.

Grammy was the first to offer a hug, and with a tear in her eye, she said, "Joe, you are one of us now. I love you. You better treat my granddaughter well or else." She raised a playful fist toward him. She then pulled out a chocolate-crème-filled doughnut. "Sorry, the bakery wasn't open, and this is the best I could do with no notice, Joseph." Grammy raised an eyebrow at him.

Joe laughed and took the doughnut from Grammy. "This will do." He turned and said, "Well, shall we? 'Can't cut the cake, but we can share the doughnut." They all laughed.

On the way to the restaurant to have a special dinner that Joe had arranged for, she rested her head on his shoulder in the front of their

1978 Chevy Caprice. They held hands the whole way. He asked her, "Were you surprised?"

She answered, "Of course, I did not see that coming, and the timing couldn't have been more perfect. You know how much I love Christmastime, and having my grandmother and mother there meant a lot to me. Thank you for being you." She laid her head back down.

Loud horns were screaming as Joe came back from his daydream and noticed the truck coming through the intersection. *That was close,* he thought. *This is going to be challenging, to say the least. How can you go back when you've lost something so precious?* He began to pull into the parking deck at the airport.

CHAPTER TWELVE

A S SEBASTIAN FOLLOWED his father down the winding staircase, he could hear more chanting. He noticed a small opening in the wall, a perfect place to hide and watch. Sebastian could only see the candles and a small opening between the men's robes. He could just see something that looked like an altar of some sort and a goblet encrusted with jewels. A young woman was sitting there in a white robe; they continued to chant over her, and then one of the men pulled out a delicate small jewel-encrusted scalpel and laid it next to the goblet. Another man seemed to bless or chant over the cup and blade.

The hooded man who appeared to be in charge then came up, emptied a vial of liquid into a glass, and handed it to the young woman. "Please drink this." She shook her head no. He then whispered, "I could make you do it, but it needs to be done on your own free will. So I'll ask you one more time, please drink it."

As he handed it to her again, another hooded man stepped toward her to encourage her to drink it. She hesitantly took the glass and drank the contents. She coughed and seemed to be choking, and then there was silence. *Oh no, was she dead*, Sebastian thought. *No, my father could be a stern man, but I do not believe that he could kill someone.* This was a lot for Sebastian to process.

They then lifted her limp body onto the altar next to the goblet and blade. The hooded man in charge began to chant again, and all the other man knelt down as if to pray, their heads bowed to the floor. The hooded man then proceeded to cut her wrists and let her blood drain into the goblet. As one of the assistants held the goblet to gather the blood, the hooded man then started to carve what looked like a strange symbol on her chest. Sebastian was too far away to see what it was. Just then, the assistant applied a bandage and held pressure on the woman's wrist wounds. They were so precise that they obviously knew what they were doing.

All the men then lifted their heads as the hooded man drank from the goblet and chanted; he then passed it around to each one of the men, who took a sip of the young woman's blood. *How gross*, Sebastian thought. *But these were the most powerful men I knew of, so there has to be a reason they were doing this.*

The members then started to stand; each grabbed a lit candle again and got back in line. This was his cue to exit; he ran up the stairs through the library and straight to his room. What did he just witness? He was confused, scared, and a little excited. Ms. Charlotte must have heard him run upstairs because she knocked gently on his door and said, "Sebastian, are you OK?" He replied yes as he quickly got back in bed.

That was quick, he thought. What would she have done if she found him running back to his room? How would he have explained it to her? Did she have any idea this was going on at all or about this secret room below the estate? The questions running through his head now would not let him sleep.

The next morning at breakfast, Johnathon was extremely quiet. Sebastian tried not to make much eye contact with him as he felt like his father would figure out what he had witnessed the night before. Sebastian quickly ate his breakfast and asked to be excused. "Father, I'm still not feeling well. May I be excused?"

"Yes, Sebastian, you may. Make sure you attend to your studies. Your headmaster told me your year-end tests were coming up. You know how important it is to get the best grades. You will need them to get into the Boy's Academy, which is the best secondary school in this country. If you are going anywhere in life, you must get into this school. I will only have the best of everything, Sebastian. That includes you having the best grades. No excuses!"

"Yes, Father, I am aware, and I have been studying, especially math. I will make you proud, I promise." He headed up to his room to study. "Someday I will join them!" He just felt it deep in his core; this would be his destiny.

TRACY ANNE BERTINI

CHAPTER THIRTEEN

M IKE WALKED OUT onto the runway toward the private
jet; he had gotten there with just enough time to see the
mahogany coffin being loaded into the plane while Jeff and Sebastian
stood and watched. Mike stopped for a moment out of respect. Once
it was on board, he walked over and extended his condolences to Jeff.
"I'm so sorry she didn't get to go home and visit with her family. That
is all she talked about for the last year—how she just had to figure out
a way to get home, time was going too fast, and it had been way too
long, she would tell me."

"Thank you for coming with me, Mike. I know it would've meant
the world to Stacy. She would appreciate you both helping me through
all of this. She was always so worried about everyone else."

Sebastian motioned to the stairs of the plane. "Gentlemen, shall
we?" he asked.

"Oh yes, thanks," Jeff said. The three men boarded the plane.

The plane was beautiful, from the soft leather chairs to the stunning
artwork that adorned the walls behind an enormous desk. "This is my
mobile command center," Sebastian joked. "Make yourself at home. I'm
going to check on the flight plan with the pilot and see how the weather
will be for our flight. There is a stocked fridge just on the other side
of the wall, if you need anything before our flight attendants arrive."

"Great, thanks, Sebastian," they both said. Mike and Jeff began
to make small talk as Sebastian headed to the cockpit, where he was
welcomed by the pilot.

"Good afternoon, sir. Here is the flight plan, and it looks like we
will have great weather for flying. We should reach Georgia in just over
two hours and fifteen minutes."

"Excellent," Sebastian responded. "We will be taking off on time then?"

"Yes, sir. In fact, they just finished fueling and pulled the stairs away, so we are ready to taxi. If you wouldn't mind taking your seat and fastening your seat belt, we will be on our way."

"Perfect. Keep me abreast of any changes, if they come up."

"Of course, sir," the pilot said as he turned and started to go over the instruments and start the engines.

Sebastian walked back to the cabin. "We are all set to take off if you would please fasten your seat belts so we can proceed."

"No problem," Mike said. "So, Sebastian, have you had a chance to review the latest lab tests that Kevin and I sent over?"

"Yes, I have," he said with a smile. "Excellent work. I believe the meeting with the FDA and USDA will go in our favor. This trip is for Stacy, not work. We have plenty of time to discuss business later."

The pilot came over the PA speaker. "Gentlemen, welcome aboard Mr. Tutworth's jet. We are cleared for takeoff. We should be arriving in Atlanta in just over two hours. Sit back, relax, and leave the flying to me. We have great weather for our flight today. Here we go." As the plane gained speed, Mike watched out the window as his beloved Colorado began to get smaller and smaller the higher they went into the air.

The flight attendant came through the door once they were at their cruising altitude. "Can I get you gentlemen anything?" she asked. Jeff asked for coffee; he hadn't slept much overnight. "Absolutely. Can I get anyone else anything?"

"I'll take a Tito's and Sprite," Mike replied.

"OK, and the usual for you, sir?"

Sebastian nodded and said, "Thank you." He had impeccable manners. Mike remembered him saying he had a class on etiquette at the boarding school where he attended high school.

"Jeff, what do you think of the florist? Was she helpful? Did the funeral director take care of the plans and walk you through everything?" Sebastian asked.

Jeff was staring out the window and was in a far-off place. "Hey, Jeff, Sebastian is talking to you." Mike reached over and touched his arm. Jeff jumped. "It's OK, Jeff. It's just me. Are you OK?" Mike was concerned about him. How would he get through this emotionally, and what was he going to do for money?

Sebastian looked at Jeff and said, "Jeff, I want you to consider working for me. I can have something set up for you in a few weeks after you get back from Georgia. I could use you as a driver or part of my security team. Please think it over. It is not out of pity. I mentioned it to Stacy many times. She didn't want you to feel it was a handout, so she always told me 'no, thank you.' I saw a copy of your résumé when she was editing it for you and noticed you had done some security work in the past and had raving references. I would be elated if you would join us."

Jeff looked at Mike as if for a sign. Mike nodded yes. "All right, thank you, sir. I don't know how to repay all your kindness, sir. All I can say is thank you from the bottom of my heart."

"Please call me Sebastian," he said. "Well, I have a formal contract drawn up, and we can get it signed. I will start your salary effective immediately. Your start date will be in three weeks. Will that be enough time to get affairs settled?"

"I am speechless. You do not have to start paying me before I even do the job," Jeff quickly stated.

"I will not hear another word about it. It is done. Welcome aboard." He extended his hand and firmly shook Jeff's hand. Sebastian then pulled out his phone, called his attorney, and told him to send over the documents for Jeff's approval.

The pilot came over the PA speaker and said, "All right, gentlemen, we have caught one hell of a tailwind and are expected to arrive in Atlanta thirty minutes early. I will keep you posted as we get ready for landing. Also, we will be landing on a private runway at the airport to avoid the red tape associated with the virus outbreak."

Mike looked at Sebastian. "It's getting worse, isn't it?"

"Yes, it is, Mike. They have suspended most flights to and from Denver and Atlanta."

Mike quickly thought about Joe, who was awaiting his flight right now in Denver. "Is there a way to find out which flights are still scheduled to leave?" he asked Sebastian.

"I'm not sure, Mike. Why? Is there a problem?"

"Joe was supposed to fly out this afternoon to make the funeral as well," Mike stated.

"Why didn't you invite him to come with us? We had plenty of room as you can see," Sebastian asked.

"I honestly didn't even think of it," he replied.

"Let me make a few calls when we land, and I'll see if I can get any information."

"That would be great. I know it would mean a lot to Stacy's family if he was there. He used to live in Georgia, and he was pretty close to Stacy's brother, and of course, then he became close to Stacy's whole family. I know his wife was very close to them as well."

The pilot came over the PA system one last time. "OK, gentlemen, please take your seats and fasten your safety belts as we are making the approach to Hartsfield-Jackson now."

Buzz decided to stop by the diner and check on things while Joe was gone. He pulled up and parked his car. He entered and was greeted promptly. "Hey, Buzz, how are things? 'Haven't seen you lately. Things at the brewery must be busy."

"Oh yeah, everybody loves beer and wings." He laughed. "I promised Joe I would come by and check on things while he's gone for the funeral."

"He said you would be," the waitress added. "Well, while you're here, can I get some of that meat loaf you love? Come on, you know you want some."

"Ah, what the hell!" Buzz said. "Sure, I'll have some. Thanks."

She headed back to the kitchen, put a ticket up, and called, "Order up! Meat loaf special for Buzz. Make it snappy."

Buzz sat down in the corner booth; this was his favorite booth because you could see the whole diner and two out of the three sides of the parking lot. The waitress brought over his plate and a drink. "Here you go. Enjoy. Let me know if I can get you anything else."

TRACY ANNE BERTINI

"Thanks. I'm good, just going to sit here and enjoy my food." He saw the local law enforcement enter and order coffees to go.

One of the deputies saw Buzz and walked over. "Hey, Buzz, how are you doing tonight?"

"Pretty good, Officer, and you?" Buzz replied.

"Well, we are kind of busy backing up the Denver force with all the virus stuff. We are mostly just helping transport patients to the quarantine sites."

"Officer, can I ask you where they are quarantining?"

"I'm not sure. We haven't transported yet. Tonight is our first night on standby for it, hence the extra coffee this evening. Don't worry, Buzz, I'm sure they will have this figured out soon enough."

"I don't know, sir. I think there is a lot more to all of this. I can't put my finger on it, but it stinks, really reeks. No one will make me go to any quarantined area if I get sick. I'll stay home and deal with it."

"I hear you, Buzz, but it is the best way to handle the situation, especially with it spreading so rapidly at this point."

"Well, I suppose if you want to drink that Kool-Aid, then sure, go ahead. I won't, no way, no how. My contact at the airport told me yesterday that they have noticed an awful lot of activity in the southern part of the airport. Big covered trucks are going in and out all day and all night long. That's fishy to me." The officer was looking at Buzz with that look now, so Buzz said, "Well, you don't have to listen to old Buzz. What the hell do I know anyway?" And then he smiled and began to eat his meat loaf again.

"Well, you have a great night, Buzz, and take it easy. No drinking tonight till you get home. I wouldn't want to see you again tonight, especially for that, OK, buddy?"

"Ehhh sure, that's a big ten-four," Buzz replied. He finished his dinner and headed home. "Who does he think he is? 'Don't drink till you get home, Buzz.' Actually, I don't need a babysitter. I know I enjoy a drink, but it's not like I have a problem. What's next? They will make us get scanned on our friggin' foreheads to see what our DNA says about us or to see if we've had a drink. I gotta get out of this place. This government is just getting more and more controlling every day.

Pretty soon we will have to ask permission to take a damn piss, and I'm sure they'll have someone there to collect it." Buzz often would mumble under his breath. He shook his head in disgust as he pulled into the driveway at his house.

He noticed the security light was on. "Now I have to put up with this shit! What the hell is going on?" he yelled. He grabbed a baseball bat from the trunk and walked out back where the light was coming from. "I'm warning you, I'm not in the friggin' mood for this shit. Come out now. If you don't and I find you, it ain't gonna be pretty, I promise you that!" He opened the backyard gate and walked through; looking around, he noticed everything was thrown around. It seemed like a bomb had gone off. "What the hell happened here!" He walked the perimeter of the yard, and then entered the back door. He found no one inside or out. *Who was here?*

He ran downstairs to the basement to review the security camera footage. He installed them about a year and a half ago when he noticed the gate was open. Of course, in true Buzz fashion, he took it to the extreme and told everyone who would listen that someone was following and listening to him. It was obviously CIA, FBI, or KGB. He was convinced it was one of them. The local law enforcement ignored his calls now; they gave him the whole lecture about the boy who cried wolf, which would then infuriate him as he was clearly not a boy.

He picked up his phone and called his IT contact. "Hey, man, I need you to head up this way but keep it quiet. I think I got something," Buzz stated. "When can you get here?"

CHAPTER FOURTEEN

A NYA WAS PUZZLED. Why would there be a Denver address in the book? She tried to think, and she didn't remember her grandmother ever mentioning Denver before. Anya started looking through the stacks again. *There has to be a clue in here somewhere.* She pulled out the brochure again and looked at the pillars; she felt like she had seen them before, but where? Her head was starting to hurt. *Great, a headache. Of course, now is the time my head won't cooperate,* she thought. *I'll look at this tomorrow, I guess.* Since her accident, she knew when to push it and when not to. This was not the time to push it; there had been too much stress in the last few days.

She walked into the hall and noticed the closet door open. *Did I leave that open when I was looking for stuff in there?* She would get extremely frustrated with herself at times. She noticed her phone had three missed calls from Jess. She listened to the voice mail. "Hey, girl, just checking on you. Answer your damn phone please. I want to make sure you're all right. Well, just call me back, please."

She texted Jess, "I'm good. I have a severe headache, going to lie down for a bit. I'll call you later."

As she headed upstairs, something in her gut told her not to leave all that stuff on the table; she grabbed a backpack from the closet and put all the papers, books, photos, and gun in the bag. Then she carried the bag upstairs. She placed it on the hope chest. She lay on her bed and fell asleep.

A few hours had passed, and she awoke drenched in sweat, screaming; she took a deep breath as she calmed down and realized it was a dream. This would often happen to her. *OK, Anya, breathe. It's not real. It can't hurt you. You're safe. Look around you. You are in your home, in your room. She opened* her eyes and steadied her hands as they were shaking. When she would have these dreams, she woke up feeling so alone as if she were missing something like her heart ached, but she had no idea why.

She reached for the phone and called Jess. "Hey, I'm sorry to call this late. I had another one of those dreams, and I don't know why I keep having them."

"I know, Anya. It's OK. Don't stress about it. Obviously, your mind is protecting you from something too traumatic to deal with until you are ready. Remember, the doctors did say that happens and to not be hard on yourself. You have come so far. Do you want me to come over?" Jess asked.

"No, I'm OK. I'll just do a little reading, I guess. I just don't feel like sleeping right now. Thanks, Jess. Why do you put up with all my issues?"

"Because I love you, and you're my friend. You've helped me through some tough times with your positive way of looking at things. Keep your chin up. It's OK to feel crappy sometimes. You've been through a lot, my friend."

"Good night, Jess," Anya said.

"'Night. I'll come by in the morning to check on you."

"Oh, you don't have to, Jess. I'm fine. Really, I am." She was tired of hearing about this stupid accident that she could not remember; in fact, she couldn't remember anything that happened for a significant amount of years. Jess would remind her of things as needed. All the residents knew what had happened. After her accident, her grandmother moved to the cabin full time and had Anya come and stay with her.

She awoke to hear the cows from the neighbor's farm mooing loudly; they only did this if they were disturbed. She jumped out of bed, got dressed, grabbed her shoes, and headed to her porch off the bedroom. She didn't dare put on any inside lights as she wouldn't be able to see as well as she could with them off. Opening the porch door quietly, she could hear the cows and now other farm animals making nervous noises. She remembered her grandmother saying that animals were very intuitive, that we should always pay attention to them as they would warn us when things were not right. She knew this was true and had seen it herself last year when they had tornado warnings; she recalled the animals making the same type of noises. *We did not have storms today.* She even looked down at her weather app and checked the local radar; it was clear of any storms. *So what could be causing this?*

She stepped out onto the porch and could see three black SUVs with about five lit flashlights coming her way. This was not good; after all the weird occurrences, she needed to hide. Something told her deep down inside to hide now. She grabbed a few clothing items, her phone charger, some toiletries, and her medicine into the backpack. She threw her hair up in a ponytail and grabbed her baseball hat. She texted Jess as she ran down the stairs, "Call the police when you get this! Use the Find My Friend app to give them my location. There are three SUVs."

Just then, she heard the front door lock jiggling; she was now at the bottom of the stairs. *The back door,* she thought. As she started that way, she heard footsteps walking up the stairs on the back porch. *Oh no, this was it.*

Then she remembered all those games of hide-and-go-seek with her grandmother. *The closet,* she thought. This was her only hope as it was deep, and she could hide behind some of the stuff in there. She ran in and closed the door behind her.

Just then, she heard the front door burst open. "Oh my god, they are inside, Jess. Please send help!" she added to her text. She moved to the back of the closet and pushed some clothes in front of her. She knelt down as close to the floor as she could but not before unscrewing the light bulb just enough so it wouldn't turn on if someone was to open the closet and try to switch on the light.

She could hear whispering. "I know she is here. Her jeep is outside. You head upstairs, you head outside, you head to the basement, and I'll stay here in case any of you flush her out. Go now, you fools. Time is of the essence. Don't you know that?" She heard them running up the stairs toward her room, and then she heard someone say, "She's not here!"

Coming from upstairs, someone yelled, "What do you mean she's not here! Impossible. Tear every inch of this cabin apart till you find her!

She is here, and we will find her. I am done playing cat and mouse with her. She should never have survived that accident. If I were in charge back then, she wouldn't have either! Find her. I am tired of cleaning up other people's problems and loose ends!"

Anya was shaking, and breathing deeply was not working. She lost her footing and fell back into the wall. When she hit the wall, it made a hollow sound. *What was that?* she thought. Anya took out her phone and carefully shone it at the back of the closet, and there she saw a small doorway; she opened it and crawled through.

She could hear them throwing things around in the cabin now, opening and slamming doors; the yelling was getting louder and louder. She had to go; she had no idea who they were or what they wanted, but they wanted her dead from the sounds of it. She carefully shut the small door to the closet and crept down the strange crawl space; she had no idea where it would take her, but it was away from the cabin. Right now, she wanted to be as far from the cabin as she could possibly get.

CHAPTER FIFTEEN

T HE DENVER INTERNATIONAL Airport was such a nightmare; the lines were ridiculous as Joe was trying to get to his gate for the flight to Georgia. There were men and women dressed in what looked like hazmat suits that were bright yellow. They were taking each traveler's temperature with a forehead thermometer. This was the first time Joe had seen anything like this before. As the people's temperatures were checked, they appeared to separate the travelers into two different lines. One of the lines was set up behind a yellow caution tape; there were more people in that line, almost a two-to-one ratio.

Joe waited in line behind a woman and three small children. She began to make small talk with him. She told him how they were heading to her parents' house for an extended visit. Her husband had been deployed for four months now, and the loneliness was just too much to bear. Joe quickly said, "Thank you for your family's sacrifice and your husband's service to this great country."

She smiled, looked down with a tear in her eye, and said, "Thank you. You have no idea how much that means to us. It is a sacrifice. In fact, my husband hasn't even met this little bundle. He's just turning four months next Friday."

Joe looked at the infant and said, "Well then, happy four-month birthday, buddy!" A smile glared back at him from the baby carrier.

The lines seemed to be moving superslow, but with all virus precautions, one had to expect it. Many travelers in line complained and were downright rude to both the health-care workers and the TSA officers. *I wouldn't want to trade places with any of them*, he thought.

He noticed a large man being searched and escorted into a back corridor; he was yelling something about his constitutional rights and how they would hear from his attorney and if they even knew who he was. The two elder children in line in front of Joe looked scared now with all the commotion. Joe bent down and said, "It's OK. He's just grumpy, and I know this looks scary but think of it as a video game. People wear costumes, and there are all kinds of things happening all at once. We can play a game. Let's see how many red shirts we can find, OK?" They nodded and gave him a little smile.

The mother of the children mouthed "thank you" to him. He smiled at her and said, "No problem." Joe loved children; most everyone who knew him said he was just a big kid himself, always laughing and joking.

He looked down at his watch and noticed it was just about 2:15 p.m. At this rate, there was no way he would make his flight to Georgia. The funeral wasn't for a few days, so he had plenty of time; he was going early to attend to some personal business he had been avoiding.

One of the men in a yellow suit came over and attempted to take one of the children's temp. He said to the woman in the other suit, "He's got it."

He then proceeded to tell the mother, "We need to quarantine your boy." He grabbed the child, ripping his hand from his mother's grasp.

The mother screamed out in horror, "He was just at the doctor's office yesterday! There is no way he is sick. Please retake it." The man just continued to pull the boy forcefully from his mother's hand. The mother cried and tried to remain calm and reason with him. Now because of the commotion, the TSA officers had come over and told her that her son needed to go with or without her.

How could something like this be happening in our country? What the heck was going on? Joe stepped toward the man in the yellow suit and kindly asked him, "Come on, man, could you just retake the boy's temperature? I'm sure if he truly has a fever, his mom would go with you peacefully. Everyone is on edge with the virus and the quarantine procedures. We haven't seen anything like this here in the U.S. in our lifetime."

The man looked and Joe and said, "We do not have time to double-check every reading. Step aside, sir, or you can personally escort this family to quarantine." Joe did not have time to be messing around with quarantine; he had to get to Georgia.

The mother looked at him and said, "Please, sir, you have been so kind to my children as we have been waiting. Their dad isn't here to look out for them. Will you?"

The man in the yellow suit ran the thermometer over Joe's forehead. "You're free to proceed." He nudged him forward as they were taking the woman and her children to the other line.

Joe couldn't help but notice the mural that was painted on the wall right above where they had taped off. It was as if it were a foreshadowing of what was about to happen. He had seen the famous eerie murals on the Internet but generally, when flying, didn't pay much attention to them as he was usually rushing to a flight or happy to be home. This mural was incredibly vivid as it depicted a soldier in a gas mask with an assault rifle in one hand and a machete piercing through a dove in the other.

There was a long line of sobbing women holding what appeared to be dead children. As he looked down from the mural, he noticed the group in the area was mostly the elderly, women, and children. *That was odd*, he thought. Something didn't feel right. He remembered reading about the four murals and thought it was almost grotesque.

"Excuse me, sir," he motioned to a TSA officer.

The man walked over. "Yes," he answered.

Joe asked, "What happens to that group? Where is the quarantine area?"

The TSA officer looked at Joe, stepped back, and in a loud voice as if to let others hear him said, "Sir, these citizens will be taken to the quarantine area that has been set up and will be comfortably taken care of until they have passed the gestation period of the virus." Then when everyone seemed to go back to talking, looking at their phones, and ignoring him again, he leaned in toward Joe. "Man, I don't know what's going on, but they are not safe. I haven't seen one damn person come back from the quarantine."

Joe looked back up and saw the mother and children crying and standing in the mass of individuals. He also noticed not one of them in that group was sneezing or coughing, which didn't make sense at all. The first half of that group was now directed to walk into a hall; this airport was known for all the tunnels and secret buildings. There were some tears, but for the most part, everyone went willingly. This was literally a scene out of one of those end-of-the-world movies with families splitting up and saying, "I'll see you soon. I love you."

Joe was becoming very unsettled as he looked at the flight board and saw all the flights change to *canceled*. The first group was now all the way through the door; right near the door was a strange statue of a gargoyle sitting in a suitcase. *This day was getting weirder and weirder*, he thought.

A few moments later, the same TSA officer came over and said, "Hey, man, if you are going to help them, you only have about thirty minutes. Those doors open every thirty minutes." Then he backed up. "Sir, you'll have to come with me. Please step out of line. I'll need you to stand over there while I conduct a search of your luggage. This is just standard procedure. Is there anything in your luggage I should be aware of?"

Joe looked at his bag and handed it to him. "No, sir, nothing but clothes, toiletries, and some legal documents." He gave the bag to the TSA officer as they walked about a hundred feet from the crowded line.

"OK, this is how it's going to go. I'm going to search your bag and give you some info. What you do with it is your business. Nod if you agree." Joe nodded. "OK, this is what I know. Just over the last forty-eight hours, those yellow-suit dudes have taken over seventy-five thousand people through those doors. Not one has come back up. They are not just U.S. citizens either. Some of them can't speak a lick of English. There have to be laws against something like this, I would think. OK, sir, I am going to open your bag now. Please stay behind the blue line," he said in a loud voice.

He continued. "So last night, just after midnight, a buddy and I were on our smoke break. We sneak one around that time. We have a spot around back near the Dumpsters. Usually, that area is only used during daytime deliveries for supplies for this terminal. But here's the thing: large military-type trucks were coming and going, and I don't know, but I swore I heard crying." He backed up. "Sir, are you aware you cannot bring this mouthwash aboard the plane? It is clearly over 3.4 ounces. I'm going to have to test it."

Joe went along with him. "Oh, right, sorry. I was in a rush this morning. Yes please, by all means, check it."

The TSA officer proceeded to pull out some litmus paper and poured some of the mouthwash over it. "OK, I put some photos in your suitcase. Take a look at it, man. It's bad stuff. That little family you were talking to is in danger for sure. My shift ends in about an hour, but they will be sent down that hall before then, so are you in?" he asked Joe. "The reason I approached you was I saw how you were with that family. They are complete strangers to you, and I noticed when we were checking IDs you also hold a CDL A license. Is that correct?"

"Yes, yes, I do. What can I do to help?" Joe asked.

"Just make enough of a stink that they send you with them. I'll meet you as soon as I get off my shift. From what we can tell, they are using the buildings that were buried to hold the people as their 'quarantine' area. Man, it's about 120 feet underground, no windows and only one way in and one way out. Sir, here is your bag. You are free to go to your flight. Have a nice day."

Joe then started to cough loudly and pretended to sneeze to get the attention of the yellow-suit man. The two in yellow suits turned toward him and began to walk over. "Sir, will you please come with us?" the man in the yellow suit asked Joe. They escorted him to the area with the caution tape.

Joe said, "Yes, I'm actually not feeling well all of a sudden."

CHAPTER SIXTEEN

THEY LANDED IN Atlanta and were still on the runway as the plane came to a stop. The pilot came over the PA system. "Gentlemen, welcome to Atlanta. It is a muggy eighty-six degrees today. Just give us a few moments to get everything situated, and we will get you on your way."

Sebastian pressed the button on the two-way speaker and said, "Excellent. Thank you for another beautiful flight."

He then pulled out his phone and asked Mike, "Do you know Joe's flight number per chance?"

Mike said, "Let me check my texts. Yes, here it is, flight 155."

"This is Mr. Sebastian Tutworth. Yes, that Tutworth."

The voice on the other side of the line said, "Well, good afternoon, Mr. Tutworth. It is a pleasure to speak with you finally. What can I do for you today, sir?"

"I have a good friend of mine who may be getting tied up in all the red tape at the airport. He is on flight 155. I need for him to be sent through swiftly as we expect him in Atlanta posthaste. His name is Joe—"

"Yes, sir," the voice interrupted. "I have him right here on the passenger list. Joe, last name—well, he is the only Joe on the passenger list." He laughed. "Let me call TSA and see if we can locate him."

"I do appreciate your help," Sebastian told the person on the phone. I can be reached directly at this phone number when his whereabouts is located."

"Sir, it looks like they have canceled all the flights from Denver for the next forty-eight hours. It seems the virus infection has gotten out of control according to this memo from the CDC and FAA. I am sorry," he said.

"Not a problem. I will be sending my private jet back to get him. Please locate him and show him to the VIP lounge to wait for the flight."

"Oh, of course, sir, I will personally take care of it."

"Thank you, and please call me when you locate him," Sebastian said and hung up. "I have them looking for Joe now. We should hear something soon."

The jet door opened, and the men departed the plane as Stacy's coffin was waiting at the bottom of the stairs. Jeff walked over and rubbed the mahogany coffin. "You're home, Stacy. You're home." Mike put his arm around Jeff's back and walked him to the car that was waiting for them.

"This car will take us to the hotel. And, Jeff, you will head to the house of Stacy's parents. The other car will take Stacy to the funeral home."

Jeff nodded. "Thank you, Sebastian." They got into the car and headed up I-85 toward Cumming. This was the city her family lived in; Stacy grew up here. "Wow, I don't miss this," said Jeff as they hit the traffic around Spaghetti Junction. "'Seems even worse than I remember."

"Oh, you have no idea," Mike said. "I had been coming back and forth for the last few years while I was the regional executive chef. This area has grown so much in the past five to seven years. There are parts that I almost don't recognize. You and Joe used to live in Cumming, right?"

"Yes," Jeff responded. "But Joe and his wife moved to Dawsonville a couple of years after his wife's accident. They liked being closer to the mountains and the slower pace."

"That's what I had thought," Mike said. "It is nice up there. Joe doesn't talk about Georgia. He's told me the story about his wife but said it's just hard to think about it. He has been putting off coming back to deal with the divorce papers. I don't know how he has lived with it. It's one thing to lose someone but the thought of—"

Just then, Sebastian's phone rang. "Excuse me, gentlemen. Hello," he answered. "OK, well, please keep abreast of the situation." He addressed the men. "It seems they have completely canceled all flights from Denver to anywhere. Joe was going through TSA when he was pulled for an inspection, and then he somehow ended with a group of people to be quarantined. I have my men working on it now. They will get to the bottom of it soon."

They pulled up Doc Bramblett Road to the house of Stacy's parents and pulled into the driveway. The car stopped, and the driver opened Jeff's door. "Sir, we have arrived." Jeff looked down at his hands, took a deep breath, and stepped out.

There stood Stacy's sister, her husband, Stacy's father, and both her niece and nephew. "Oh, Jeff, we are so glad you're home." They hugged him one by one.

"Oh, I'm so sorry. Please let me introduce Mr. Sebastian Tutworth. If it weren't for him, we would not have been able to get Stacy home. We all owe him an enormous debt of gratitude."

Stacy's father extended his hand and shook Sebastian's, saying, "Thank you, sir, for your kindness toward our family. It humbles us."

Meanwhile, at the airport, Joe joined the group of people escorted down the long hallway; he had caught back up with the mother and her children. "Are you all OK?" he asked.

"Yes, just scared," she replied. They walked for at least half of a mile and then got into open freight elevators.

One of the suited yellow men said, "This one is going to building 5."

"OK, and the other group?" The worker asked.

"That group?" He chuckled. "They are headed to building 3."

"Oh boy, OK," he replied. Joe was trying to listen to their discussion; it seemed going to building 5 was much better than building 3 from their reactions. He turned and looked around and tried to pay attention to the details of this tunnel.

They finally reached the bottom, and the elevator stopped. "OK," the man in the suit said. "Go through the doors and stay to the right, please. You will make two lines. Proceed to the table where you will have your vitals taken and documented. We will draw a blood sample, and you will be given a change of clothes. Once we have you checked in and registered, you will be escorted to the bunks and common areas, where you will be able to rest. We run a tight ship down here as we have to, with the number of people who are here receiving treatment. You will be meeting with the medical staff two times per week for an exam. Your vitals will be monitored and documented every few hours by our nursing staff."

A few hands went into the air. "Please hold all question. I'm sure we will answer them in due time. My name is Sergeant Nichols. My team and I are in charge here. So please let's all try to stick to the program and schedule to make everyone's time here easier. OK, we are going to get started. Please form two lines and proceed forward as you are called."

Joe quickly began to notice they were calling names from a roster of some sort. *What? How could they have already known who was ill that quick?* Joe thought. He was puzzled. Down the hall were bright lights and a large room where everyone was heading after getting registered.

As he was walking in line, he noticed a sign stating, "Unfortunately, cell service is insufficient, but you would have the opportunity to make a call as you earned privileges." *What the hell did that mean? What was this place? Clearly, no one here was sick. The other group was clearly the sick bunch.*

Joe got to the table, being last in line. "Sir, what is your name?"

He started to say, "Joe."

Just then, Sergeant Nichols came over. "You, sir, are not supposed to be here, period. You will be escorted back upstairs and on your way."

Joe asked, "But what about everyone else? How did they know their names? And they are not sick. What's going on here?"

The last thing he felt was the cold, hard sting of the back of a gun at the base of his head. "Lights out. Next time, you should listen to what you are told. Good night." The other men dragged Joe's helpless body out of a tunnel. Joe woke up on the jet with a cold cloth on his forehead.

The flight attendant walked over and handed him a ginger ale and some saltines. "Well, Joe, you had one nasty fall. There is a big gash on the back of your head, but the doc stitched you up. Eat something. It will settle your stomach. We are set to arrive in Atlanta in about an hour."

"I thought the flights are canceled," Joe said.

"They are, but Mr. Tutworth arranged for his jet to come and bring you to Atlanta."

CHAPTER SEVENTEEN

B UZZ HEARD THE knock at the door, grabbed his gun, and proceeded to open it. "Man, what took you so long?" Buzz asked. "I've pulled the footage from my security cameras. You are not going to believe it. There were four men here dressed in black suits. They were apparently looking for something."

"All right, Buzz, let's see what happened. I just need to upload the footage to my computer, and then we can zoom it in and get some answers. So what has been going on at the airport?" the IT man asked.

Buzz replied, "I'm trying to get to the bottom of it. From what I can tell, there is some kind of military deployment or mission. The trucks that have been coming and going used to be for transporting soldiers in WWII. My guess would be they are moving troops into place and don't want anyone to know about it yet."

"Why would they do that, Buzz?"

"To strategically put troops in place before they are needed," Buzz answered.

"It looks like the upload is done. Do you want me to run it through my facial recognition program to see if we get a hit?"

"Yes, let's be sure to check all the databases."

"Buzz, you're not saying that the military is sending troops to the airport in advance of a what? A mission? To manage the quarantine? Martial law?"

"I haven't figured it out yet. All I know for sure is that the military equipment is arriving in large numbers. It's strategic. They do not move expensive equipment into an area without a well-thought-out plan," Buzz explained.

"I agree with you, Buzz, but you know, with all the people missing in the area, it is concerning, to say the least."

"It is, but I've been preparing for this for years. I've warned everyone, but of course, people just think old Buzz is crazy. Well, we will see who is crazy now. I'm heading to the airport tonight to do some recon and access the situation. My contact there is a TSA officer. We go way back to our army days. A true patriot and an all-around great guy. If anything is about to go down, he will have an idea." Buzz often would call on his platoon as they had been through hell and back together. "Do you want to come tonight?" He asked.

"Yes, that sounds like a plan." Buzz answered. "Hey, Buzz, I'm going to take these files with me. They are taking forever to run through the program. I have a few things to get ready if we are headed out there tonight."

"All right, man, if you find anything, which I doubt you will, knowing these dicks the way I do, call me right away. I'm heading out after I swing by my bunker. Listen, be prepared for anything tonight. I have no idea what we will find." Buzz headed through the mountains and, about an hour later, arrived at his bunker. He had become quite the doomsday prepper. Unless you knew the bunker was there through the cave, it was completely hidden in plain sight. He looked around to make sure he hadn't been followed. No one or nothing was around for miles. "Perfect, let's get busy!"

He entered the cave and walked through the narrow crevice naturally made in the rock. There was a large steel door behind a wall of moss. Buzz had found this place years ago and decided it was the perfect location to keep his supplies. As he walked through the door, he headed right to the metal cabinet where he kept a substantial arsenal. Buzz grabbed a duffel bag of supplies, including enough ammo and guns for a zombie apocalypse. "That should just about do it!" he said. He grabbed the old two-way radio too. He then added to his supplies a couple of gas masks and a hazmat suit.

Buzz's phone started to ring. "Hello?"

The voice on the other end said, "Buzz, I can't talk long, but it's happening. We need to put things in place now, no time to waste! When will you be here? I have a feeling that the quarantines are actually a front for something much more sinister."

"I have the same feeling. I'm getting the supplies we need, and then I'm on my way. Are we still meeting in the back?" he asked.

"Yes, my break is at 11:00 p.m. Make sure you're here by then!"

"I'll be there!" Buzz made sure to cover and lock everything in the bunker. On his way out, he went into the storage room and counted the medical supplies and food rations he had been slowly stockpiling over the last year. He grabbed some antibiotics before turning off the light and leaving the safety of the bunker. Packing up the car, he could see the sun starting to set over the Rockies. "I gotta get going. I got things to do!" Poor Buzz had no idea of the things he would be doing and the mess that waited at the airport for him.

TRACY ANNE BERTINI

CHAPTER EIGHTEEN

ANYA QUICKLY CRAWLED down the dark passageway to who knew where. She stopped for a quick moment to look at her phone. Did Jess even get her text? Was help on the way? "No service." She had no choice but to continue down the tunnel.

There was a fork in the tunnel. *Which way should I go?* she quickly thought. Anya could see a faint light in the distance, down the tunnel on the right. *I'll head down that one and see where the light is coming from. Hopefully, someone would be there to help.* The passage was just a hole dug out of the earth. The Georgia clay was cold as she crawled further down the tunnel. Anya would occasionally stop to wipe away a spiderweb or to remove a tree root that would tear at her pants. *Finally, the lit opening.* She prayed someone would be there; she carefully used her phone's camera to use it as a mirror to view the area. No one was there; she could see an old wooden table with a small lamp on it, a chair, a few books, and a door on the other side of the room.

As she started to climb out of the tunnel, her leg got caught on the metal grate that covered the opening. The blood began to run down her pant leg; she could feel the burning sting from the torn flesh on her thigh. Holding back tears, she jumped down from the opening and let out a gasp as she landed on the dirt floor. She pulled the torn pant leg away from the wound to access the injury; it was about six inches long and jagged. She tore the rest of the pant leg off and used some bottled water to clean away the dirt from the wound. Then she fastened the pant leg around her thigh above the wound to slow the bleeding.

Looking around the room, she pulled the chair over to the table; as she sat, she looked at the books. There was one book that caught her eye. *There it is again, the sand dollar, on the leather spine of the book. That has to be important.* She grabbed the book and placed it in her backpack with the other things she had brought along. Now was not the time to stop and take a look.

After resting for a few moments, the blood had slowed down, and she headed toward the door. Slowly, she opened it. *Another dark hallway, perfect,* she thought.

"At least I can stand and walk in this one," she said like anyone could hear her. No one even knew where she was; her GPS wasn't even working on her phone, so even if Jess did get the message, there was no way to locate her. Things had gone from bad to much worse. She pulled out her phone again and used her step counter; at least she would have some kind of idea how far she had walked away from the cabin to alert someone when she got a signal. According to her phone, she had been gone for over six hours already; it felt like she had been walking for days all alone, not knowing where she was headed.

Her leg was swelling, and the pain was getting to her, but she didn't have time to think about it right now; she had to continue to push. Since Anya's accident, she had been through a lot of physical therapy and strength training and did a lot of meditation and yoga to control the chronic pain. She was getting tired; she needed to rest, but when would this tunnel end? Her head was starting to get foggy; she felt like she had done this walk before, but there was no way. She had no idea these tunnels even existed.

Finally, she came to another door; this was metal, and it looked like an old bunker door. There was a sign on the door that was almost unrecognizable from the thick layer of dirt on it. She took the other piece of the pant leg and wiped the sign as clean as she could. The sign read, "Caution: This is a restricted zone. Any unauthorized persons will face military prosecution for criminal trespassing." She also saw the sign with the radioactive symbol on it. This felt so familiar to her as if it had happened before.

Anya opened the heavy door and walked up the cement stairs. It was the middle of the night, and the sky was filled with bright stars. The area was heavily wooded, but the moon was big and bright; it illuminated the outlines of a few buildings. They were abandoned for sure. She decided to rest for the night; she would continue after the sun came up. There was a building at the top of a small hill. *That would do for shelter tonight.*

Anya walked up the hill and entered the building; there was a staircase that went both up and down. The higher viewpoint she had, the better in case she was followed. The stairs that went down had been flooded at the bottom, and there was no way she was doing that in the middle of the night. She headed upstairs toward the roof; the pain was so intense that she felt as if she may pass out. Once on the roof, she headed over to the ductwork and lay just beneath the hood to provide some shelter from any elements just in case. She sat down, opened her bag, and pulled out a hoodie, a bottle of water, a protein bar, and a blanket. After eating the bar and drinking the water, she put the hoodie on, wrapped herself in the blanket, and nodded off.

Tonight her dreams were incredibly vivid. Leaving Dawson Forest, he ran beside Anya as they both were running for their lives. She was falling behind, but he never left her side. Reaching for her hand, they continued to run toward the Nissan Pathfinder. "Oh my god, hurry!" she yelled. "They are right behind us."

"I know, baby. Just stay calm. We are going to be OK," he responded. The tree limbs from the old pine trees smacked their bodies and stung with each hit, tearing through their skin. The sun was setting.

Gunshots rang out through the woods. The bullet flew by his head and lodged in the tree next to them. "That was close," he said. "Listen, sweetie, we are going to have to split up. There is no way we can get to the truck. I will run off the other way and get them to follow me. You run for the truck. You know what to do. All the proof is in the trunk. I'll meet you back at the cabin. After you get the package to the Forsyth County Sheriff's Office, make sure to ask for Sergeant Jackson. He is expecting us and will know what to do. We are so close, baby. It will be over soon. Here, take the Glock nineteen with you. I'll keep the twenty with me. We just need to get to the other side of that hill, and I will run back toward the woods. You go for the truck."

"I don't want to go. We can both make it. I know we can," she replied. "You just have to stay positive. We can't split up!"

They could hear the voices getting closer. "You might as well just give up. We will catch you, and you will die. You have to know this is not going to end well for either of you. This plan has been in the works for hundreds of years, and the likes of you will not get in the way. You cannot stop this!" More shots came in their direction. They echoed each time, but with all the hunting done in this area, no one would even be bothered by the gunshots. They were on their own in the woods. These men were not military but expertly trained nonetheless. The shots were getting closer; time was running out. They had to make their move now.

"No matter what happens, you know I love you more than anything, baby. Be strong." He grabbed her in a tight embrace and kissed her deeply as tears ran down both of their faces.

"I love you too. Don't make me do this. Let's just stay together," she pleaded.

"Now run, sweetheart, run!" he yelled as he pushed her in the direction of the truck while firing the twenty repeatedly in the direction of the men, who were gaining on him. The men stopped for only a moment as they noticed him running in the other direction. They turned toward the shots and ran after him. His plan had worked; she was free to run to the truck quickly.

As she approached the SUV, she grabbed the keys from her pocket, hit the key fob to unlock the door, swung open the door, and jumped in. She only caught her breath for a brief moment and then started the vehicle. Heading out of the Dawson Forest, she couldn't help but notice no armed guards were at the gate. She turned right onto Highway 9, heading south toward Forsyth County. Passing Bannister Road, she saw headlights quickly gaining on her. When she would speed up, they would catch up to her. The bumper of the black sedan nudged the bumper of her silver Pathfinder. *God, if you're listening, please get me to Sergeant Jackson*, she prayed.

The road was dark and windy. Now two large trucks pulled out in front of her at Highway 369, and shots were fired from the first vehicles. There was no way she would get out of this. The last thing she remembered was headlights coming right toward her; she briefly looked down at the clock and saw the time—6:33 p.m.—and then nothing.

Anya woke up from her dream in a cold sweat again, gasping for air, just as the sun was rising over the tree line. She sat for a moment just to catch her breath. "Why do I keep having these dreams? They seem all too real, but wait, I can remember this one, every detail. This does not happen." Her neurologist said that memories may come back at any time; there was no rhyme or reason to it. Could this be a real memory and not a dream? If it was, maybe she didn't want to remember. This was a scary thought, but she didn't have time to think about it now. She had to figure out how to get out of here and get word to Jess.

CHAPTER NINETEEN

IT WAS ABOUT 7:00 a.m., and Mike was sitting in the hotel lobby, drinking his coffee and reading the newspaper, waiting for Joe to come down from his room. They had a lot to catch up on. Joe didn't get settled till late last night, so Mike wanted him to rest. His cell phone rang; it was Joe. "Hey, man, are you already downstairs?" he asked.

"Yeah, I've been down here for about twenty minutes. You coming down? OK, see you soon." Mike hung up and motioned to the waitress. "We are ready for our table now, and can I get another coffee for my friend? He is on his way."

"Of course." The server showed him to the table and poured the other cup of coffee. "I'll be back in a few to take your orders."

"Perfect, thank you," he answered.

A few moments later, Joe walked over to the table and sat down. "Hey, how's it going this morning? You feeling better? I heard you had a fall or something at the airport in Denver," Mike said.

"I need coffee before we get into all of that," Joe answered.

"OK, let's order, chill for a bit. We have plenty of time to catch up. I will tell you, boy, do I have one hell of a headache." They both ordered breakfast. Then they noticed the TV was talking about the virus again.

"Can you turn it up?" Joe asked the server.

"Oh sure," she replied as she turned the volume up.

"There have now been over one hundred thousand cases worldwide. It has reached a pandemic status and has no signs of letting up. The CDC is feverishly working to figure this out. The death toll has risen to approximately half of that number with another 25 percent in critical condition. Travel overseas has now been suspended to try to slow this deadly virus down. CDC spokesperson Ms. Hardy has been quoted as saying this could be the virus that wipes out a large number of human population. The CDC and the World Health Organization have compiled a board of top scientists and physicians from many countries across the globe. She also said this is now a global issue and that we must combine our resources to help in the fight against the pandemic. Only military personnel or those who are escorted by military personnel will be allowed to travel in and out of our country. The governor of each state will also be able to close their state's borders during this outbreak. Here is a list of states that have already closed their borders effective immediately until further notice: Alaska, Arizona, Colorado, Florida, Georgia." The newscaster continued to name at least twenty-nine states.

Joe turned to Mike and said, "This is getting way out of control. I guess we are stuck here for a while. I'll have to call Buzz and have him continue to look after the diner."

"So what happened at the airport?" Mike asked.

"The lines were crazy, a lot of confusion. The one thing that was really unsettling was the way it appeared they were separating people. As they were reading the thermometer readings right in front of me, they took a young boy from his mother, saying he had a fever. I saw the reading. It clearly read 98.9 degrees. They argued with his mother and forcefully took him. There was a TSA officer who started telling me all the weird things going on in the middle of the night and pretty much told me to pretend I was sick so I could be sent to the quarantine. It didn't make much sense, but then when I got to the quarantine area, it became crystal clear. They already had a list of people's names that were chosen to be pulled out of line and detained. Down in the buildings, there was no cell service. There are strange signs that said something about earning privileges to make a phone call. The whole place was creepy and run by one hard-ass of a drill sergeant. As soon as he realized my name was not on the list, I started to question what was going on, and—bam!—something hit me on the back of the head. I woke up on the jet on the way here to meet you. Something is going on. After the funeral, we can head up to the mountains and ride out this virus there."

"Now that, my friend, is a plan."

"Mike, I have a couple of errands to run before this afternoon. Do you want to come with me or hang here?" Joe asked.

"I'll hang here, I think. I'm meeting with Sebastian in an hour or two."

"OK, I'll see you a little later then. See ya."

Joe went out to the parking lot and got into the rental car. As he drove away, he couldn't help but think about his life in Georgia; this trip was already haunting him. "Call Buzz," he prompted his phone. It started to ring.

"Hello?" Buzz answered.

"Hey, it's Joe. How are things in Denver?"

"A lot is going on here, man, but we can't talk about it on the phone. The diner is excellent. The town is pretty much shut down. No one is getting in or out. You're lucky you were able to get out when you did. Someone broke into my house and trashed the yard, apparently looking for something."

"Buzz, when I was at the airport, long story short, I ended up going down into a building buried under it. That's where they are quarantining. Do you know anything about the buildings?" Joe asked.

"Hey, man, that's some heavy-duty stuff. A lot of secrets are surrounding those buildings. Listen, the phone lines aren't safe. Do you still have access to the old radio?" Buzz hoped the answer was yes.

"I mean, I know where it is. I have a couple of things to take care of, but then I can go pick it up. Can it wait a couple of hours?"

Buzz said, "Yes but not much longer. I have a feeling we are already on borrowed time."

"All right, Buzz, keep calm. I'll radio you in a few hours. Sounds like a plan?"

"That's a big ten-four, buddy. I'll talk to you soon."

Joe ended the call and took a deep breath. He continued to drive up Highway 400 to Dawsonville. *Wow, the place had changed so much since my last visit.* He almost didn't recognize it. He pulled in and parked the car. He grabbed the folder of papers from the front passenger's seat and headed in the building.

A young woman sat at the reception desk and greeted him with a big smile. "Good morning, sir. How are you today?"

"Good," he replied. "I am here to see John. I have an appointment."

Just then, John came out of his office. "Well, well, look what the cat dragged in. How have you been? It feels like ages since you've been home." John was Joe's attorney for years now, and the two had become friends. "Did you finally sign the papers? You do know you have been more than fair and have provided for her every need. I mean, what are you supposed to do in a circumstance like this?"

Joe looked down at the desk and sighed. "It was never meant to be like this. The last time I saw her, I tried to talk to her. And of course, that only upset her. She does not remember a thing. I spoke with the physician again, and they said her condition has not changed. In fact, they actually think it may be permanent." His eyes began to fill with tears at the thought of being without his girl for the rest of his life; it was almost too much to bear. "John, how fast will this all be finalized? The courts do realize she has no idea and can't comprehend what is going on, right?"

"Yes, Joe, we have to handle things like this often in the courts."

"It's just not fair to have someone ripped from you in the prime of their life. Well, I have no words. We were robbed of a future—a future we had planned, a future we deserved and worked hard for together."

John walked over to Joe. "I know, Joe, but it's time. You have to let her go. Even if you're not ready, it's time."

CHAPTER TWENTY

Y EARS HAD GONE by, and Sebastian continued to excel in business and sharpened his negotiation skills. He was a college graduate—Yale, of course. He was very proud of his accomplishments and was ready to go home and work with his father. He loaded up the rest of his belongings and headed out to the car. He had graduated with honors from Yale and had a master's degree in business and finance. His résumé and transcripts were top-notch; any company would be honored to have him on their team. Sebastian only wanted to work for one person; he wanted to prove to his father he was the man he always wanted him to be. The trip home would take a couple of days; he was ready to see the country on his way home.

As he drove across the country, he reflected on the almost love-hate relationship he had with his father. He thought, *It is all about to change.* He had grown into his body and had surgery to help him walk without being hunched over.

Sebastian was quite the catch and one of the most eligible bachelors; he was educated, cultured, a billionaire, and an excellent ballroom dancer and spoke six different languages fluently. While at school, he had a few relationships, but nothing really blossomed into anything important. He watched while the other young men went on dates and had girlfriends. Having Johnathon Tutworth as a role model in the relationship department was not all it was cracked up to be. Both Tutworths were known for their taste of exquisite things, including women. Being alone was actually how he preferred to spend his late nights. Work was his partner, which left no room for a woman. He would bring home his latest trophy to add to the collection in his head.

The night would always end the same way, a beautiful young woman being escorted home by his car service.

He looked forward to returning to the estate and getting settled in. He often wondered what Ms. Charlotte was doing; he had kept in touch over the years with her, and his heart would soar at the very thought of her. The last two years, he hadn't reached out to her. If there was any woman who could make him happy, it was her. She was always there to give him advice or just listen to how his day went. Even though Sebastian and Charlotte were eight years apart, they had become friends. He missed their talks and the feeling someone cared. She had stayed in South Carolina to be near her parents as far as he had known.

Charlotte had become a big part of his plan; she just had no idea. "The time is coming, my dear. You will be mine!" He did not take no for an answer, and he was accustomed to always getting his way. *She would make an excellent wife and mother for my heir.* He could trust her to not be snooping into his secret business. It was the perfect solution to his problem, which was to take his rightful place; he needed to be able to produce an heir. Charlotte came from good southern stock; as with everything the Tutworths owned, she would be his most prized possession. He needed to make this part of his plan flawless so everything would go perfectly.

He dialed the phone. "This is Charlotte. Leave a message and have a blessed day."

He said, "Charlotte, it's me, Sebastian. I wanted to know how you were doing, and I wanted to catch up. It has been way too long. I look forward to hearing from you soon. I will be traveling toward the Southeast soon and would love to be able to meet up."

CHAPTER TWENTY-ONE

A S JOE HEADED to pick up Mike for Stacy's viewing at the funeral home, he noticed quarantine signs on the side of Highway 400 southbound. There was a 1-800 number to call if you or a loved one showed any signs of the virus. It was ominous, to say the least, usually on these signs. You would see attorney advertisements and local restaurants, but he had never seen anything like this. Joe dialed Mike's cell. "Hey, Mike, are you ready? I can swing by and pick you now if you want."

"Sure, I'm dressed and ready. I just finished my meeting with Sebastian, and it looks like everything is on track for the project. I'm so proud of the work we have done."

"All right, Mike, that's great. I'm on my way. 'Be there in about ten minutes," Joe replied. He hung up the phone and headed toward the hotel, making a quick pit stop at the florist to order his flowers for Stacy's memorial service on Saturday.

"'Afternoon, sir. What can I help you with today?" the clerk asked.

"I need to order some flowers for a dear friend's memorial service. I think a standing spray would work."

"OK, let me see what I have in the cooler. I'll be just a minute." The clerk vanished into the back room of the florist.

As Joe waited, he noticed a missed call, but he did not recognize the phone number. His text alert went off just then. "Hey, Joe, we need to talk. Things are not looking good, and I'm really worried about her. I don't think she is going to pull through. Please, when you get this message, call me. I believe it's finally happened. I know you haven't come to terms with all that has happened but—"

"All right, sir, I have some beautiful gladiolas and roses, a few stargazer lilies."

Joe just stared at his phone. *Is it happening?* The thought of it made him sick to his stomach and terrified. Did he finally lose her for good? He often wrestled about why it happened and what he could've done to have fixed it. He made sure his wife had the best medical care and therapists and was financially provided for as well. The pain of seeing her like that was too much to bear, so after many failed attempts to try to care for her himself, he decided to spend the majority of his time in Denver at the diner instead of Georgia. He checked in on her often by phone with her caretakers, and they would send short videos of her so he could see for himself there was no change. She would never have wanted him to not live his life because she couldn't. After all, they were the best of friends and loved each other more than life itself.

He would always remember the way she looked that night at the football game, their first date. Her wavy dark brown hair and deep chocolate brown eyes, oh how he adored to look deep into them and play with her messy curls as they would fall in front of her eyes. Why couldn't he have saved her from this cruel fate? She was the one and only love of his life.

He grew up in a large loud Italian family with lots of food, drama, opinions, and dysfunction, like most. He was the third child of four. As a child, he was somewhat shy but always the funny guy. For years, he had an on-again-off-again relationship with his family; but she was constantly there in his life, always cheering him on and ready to take on the next adventure, big or small. She had saved him so many times throughout the years, but he felt he had failed her.

They had been married for almost twelve years when he came home from work with another one of his crazy ideas. "So how do you feel about moving far away? Just the two of us taking on the world, spreading our wings. It would be an adventure," he told her.

"An adventure? Really? And why would I want to do that? All my family and friends are here in Massachusetts. Besides, what kind of adventure are you talking about? Where exactly is this so-called adventure? Grammy would be heartbroken if I left."

He quickly rushed over to her, put his arms around her waist, and said, "All kidding aside, I would like to take this opportunity and see where it takes us." He had been a CDL class A driver and recently won the truck-driving championship for the state of New Hampshire for safe driving and was heading to the nationals to represent his company. "With the mud season up here and the winters, there is definitely more stability down south. So I was thinking Arizona, Texas, or Georgia. What do you say?"

"Arizona may be nice, but Georgia, what is there? Swamps?" she said with a laugh. There it was again—that smile, the wit-and-adventure girl he fell in love with at the football game years ago. "Let me talk to Grammy and see what she thinks. Is that OK?"

"Of course, my lady," he answered with a smile. Joe just wanted to get away from the drama and make a new life for the two of them.

Just then, the clerk finally raised his voice after clearing his throat. "I'm not sure where you were a moment ago, but you looked happy. I wish I had just a moment of that happiness."

"I am sorry. I guess I was daydreaming about a better time and place, lifetime ago actually," he responded. "I think the stargazers will be perfect. Can you have them delivered first thing in the morning?"

"Of course, sir, no problem, and keep a tight hold on whatever it was that makes that smile."

He left the florist and picked Mike up for the viewing. "Have you talked to Jeff yet?" Joe asked.

"No, not since yesterday. Have you?"

"I left a message for him this morning, but I figure he's busy with all the arrangements and needs to be with Stacy's family right now."

Pulling into the funeral home, Joe said, "We're here. Let's head in."

"Hey, Joe, can you give me a minute?"

"Take all the time you need. I'll be near the front door. I see Stacy's sister. I'm going to talk to her for a bit."

As Mike walked to the door, he noticed three black SUVs parked on the side of the road. He could clearly see at least two men in each of the vehicle. He had an uneasy feeling about this. He walked over to Joe. "Did you see the three SUVs over there parked? I have a funny feeling about this. Something isn't right."

CHAPTER TWENTY-TWO

ANYA COLLECTED HER belongings and repacked her backpack. She moved the makeshift bandage from her thigh to look at the wound. Most of the blood was dried, but the wound was still seeping a bit. She poured some water on it and rewrapped it with another piece of her pant leg to keep it clean. She could hear running water in the distance; she walked toward the water sounds, hoping to get her bearings.

While walking toward the river, the pain was getting worse in her leg; she looked down at her phone and still had no signal. The water sounds were getting closer as she walked through the heavily wooded area. The sun was rising in the sky, and she could see its reflection dancing on the water through the pine trees. As she got closer to the river, she had a flashback of some sort of her and the man in her dreams having a picnic near the river. The feeling of missing something was overwhelming. She reached the riverbanks and decided to walk along it in hopes she would come across someone.

Her body was getting weaker; with only limited food and water over the last twenty-four hours and the loss of blood, she felt like she would pass out anytime. It started to go black all around her, and suddenly, she collapsed to the ground. Lying lifeless in the forest, her dreams started again.

"Wait, where am I?" Everything around her was still, as if a thick, soft gray fog were engulfing her and her surroundings. Looking around, she could see and hear nothing. *Where am I?* she thought. The silence was almost deafening. She was alone.

After a few moments of silence, she found herself in a conversation but could not hear the one initiating it. It was as if they were communicating telepathically. In true Anya style, she demanded to know what was going on. *Where am I, and who the heck is behind all of this!* She would pause in her rant as if carefully listening to the voice in her head. *But I don't understand. I am not done yet! I have so much to do. What about . . .* She was silent; once again, the voice communicated with her. *No, this can't be how it ends. I'm not ready. Please give me more time. This can't be it*, she pleaded.

The voice was calm, reassuring, and unwavering; it gave her a sense of peace. The calmness and peace washed over her very soul. She continued to question what had happened and how this could truly be the end. She finally took a deep breath as she realized this really was how it was going to end.

Anya finally submitted as tears ran done her cheeks. *OK, if it is your will, I'll go.* Before she could even finish the thought, she could hear fire engines, sirens, people yelling, and a cracking metal sound; and she felt the worst pain she could have imagined. She had just been somewhere so peaceful and had felt the greatest comfort in her whole life; now what was happening?

A fireman was trying to talk to her, but it sounded like he was underwater. As she started to come to, she could finally make out many people, emergency lights, and the chaos that was happening around her. Again, the firefighter asked, "Ma'am, are you OK? Please remain calm. We are working to get you out of your vehicle. Now I need you to stay as still as possible. You have been in an automobile accident, and we are all here for you. You are about to hear a lot of noise. Don't be alarmed. We are using the Jaws of Life to extricate you from your vehicle. Can you hear me, and do you understand what is happening?"

"Where am I?" she asked.

"You are in your vehicle on Dahlonega Highway just north of Route 306. Ma'am, do you remember anything?"

"No, umm, well, I was driving down the road, and I vaguely remember lights coming toward me."

The sounds from the scene were loud and chaotic. People were running across the street back and forth for tools. "Hey, can I get a hand over here?" the police officer yelled.

TRACY ANNE BERTINI

Sitting there, so many things were running through her mind. The pain got more intense, but she was able to move her left arm. She raised it slightly to see if she could feel anything. She placed it on her stomach, and there was a pain but no blood. She then raised her hand to her head and felt the blood trickling down the left side of her face, and she realized the driver's side window was gone.

"Ma'am, I need you to stay as still as possible. I know this is overwhelming, but after we get you out onto the stretcher, we will be able to see what kind of injuries you have. Can you do that for me?" She nodded yes.

Then the EMTs came over and said, "OK, ma'am, here we go. On three, we are going to move the piece of frame from your legs. Stay very still. It may get warm on your skin. We have placed a cloth to protect you. OK, one, two, three." As he said *three*, the twisted metal whined as it was crushed in half. The driver's side was finally opened enough to fit one of the emergency workers into the passenger space with her.

"My name is Michelle. I'm just going to take your vital signs and take a peek around. Is that OK with you?" Anya was growing increasingly tired as she was in and out of consciousness. She nodded yes again. Michelle was taking her blood pressure and looking Anya over to see how they would proceed with getting her out. As her blood pressure reading was finished, Michelle yelled, "We need to get her out right now! She's dropping!"

Three other workers came over right away. "OK, Anya, can I call you that? We saw it on your driver's license."

"Yes, you can," Anya replied.

"We are going to place this collar around your neck to protect it, and then we will slide you onto this backboard. We need you to stay still. We will do all the work." The sirens were still blaring, and the emergency lights were almost hypnotic. She just wanted to sleep; her head was pounding. "OK, Anya, here we go. Can you move your right leg just slightly to the right? I will help guide it around the piece of metal."

Anya tried to move her leg; her brain was saying "move," but her leg did not move. Panic started to flood over her, she faintly said, "I can't feel my legs."

"OK, let me try something. I'm going to touch you, and you tell me when you can feel it." Michelle began to touch her toes, calves, and then leg. Still, Anya felt nothing. She looked at the other EMT and shook her head ever so slightly. "All right, so on the count of three again, we are going to turn you and lay you on the board. One, two, three." She was free from the vehicle; they quickly strapped her onto the board and strapped her head in place.

Before she knew it, she was in the ambulance rushing to the hospital. The EMTs were starting an IV and asking her questions. She was out again. She heard everyone yelling, "Anya, can you hear us? You are at the hospital. You've been in an accident. We are removing your clothing so we can examine you. Is there anyone we should call?"

She was confused; she didn't know. Was there someone she should have them call? The tears just continued to run down her face. She was alone and had no idea what happened or who, if anyone, she could call. She didn't remember a thing. These strangers were telling her she was in an accident, but shouldn't she remember that if she was? The hospital was loud and cold. The physicians came in one after another, ordering tests and reading CT scans, X-rays, and MRIs. All the chaos continued around her as she slipped to sleep again.

The next time she woke up, she was in a hospital room and wearing a hospital gown, and a nurse was taking her vitals. "Wait, what happened? Where am I?" she asked, looking at the nurse.

"Sweetheart, you were in an accident, and you are in the hospital. We are taking excellent care of you. No need to worry, your job is to get better."

Anya's voice was almost nonexistent. "Am I going to be OK? Am I going to die?" she asked the nurse.

"They are running tests and are trying to figure this all out for you. When they have some answers, the doc will come in and speak with you. Is there anyone I can call? Also, may I pray with you? I noticed the religion part of your form was blank. I don't want to make you

TRACY ANNE BERTINI

uncomfortable, but in my line of work, I've seen many miracles. And you, my dear, are in need of one."

"Yes please."

The next morning, when she woke up, a man was sitting in the chair, sleeping in the corner. *Who was that?* she thought. He didn't look familiar to her at all. She tried to sit up and knocked the nurse call button onto the floor, which made a thump as it hit the floor.

The man in the chair woke up, jumping to his feet. He rushed to the bedside. "Hey, you, are you OK? You had us all so scared! I don't know what I would've done without you."

Anya was looking at the strange man with sheer panic on her face. "Are you my doctor?" she asked.

"Well, it's good to see you still have your sense of humor, baby." As he laughed and reached to embrace her, she let out a scream, he jumped back, and the nurse ran into the room.

"What is wrong? Is everything OK? I heard a scream."

Anya said, "This strange man was sleeping in my room and then tried to hug me! I'd say there is something wrong!"

The nurse asked to speak to the man in the hall. "Anya, I'll be right back. He's going to come with me." Anya closed her eyes and fell back to sleep.

"What is going on? Why doesn't she remember me?" the man asked with tears running down his face.

"She has suffered some major injuries. It will take her some time to recover. This will be a long and bumpy road. It isn't going to be easy, but we are all here to help. Let her rest. I have opened the door to the room next to hers. Feel free to sleep in there. You can hear everything that is going on, but you won't scare her until we can work with her memory loss. In most cases, it is just temporary. The brain is a powerful thing. Just give it some time."

"OK, thanks for your help. I will take you up on that offer. I could use some rest."

Just as he got settled in the hospital room, the neurologist walked in with the MRI images. "May I come in? I'm the neurologist in charge of Anya's treatment while she is here with us. As you know, she suffered multiple major injuries and has a long road in front of her. With that being said, she is not out of the woods yet. The preliminary tests show the following injuries: She broke her talus bone in her right ankle, and she also broke her left foot and many toes. There are over sixty-eight microfractures in her lower legs, which are causing some bone marrow to seep out. Her right knee is completely shattered, and her left one is dislocated. Her right hip is slightly displaced, and the right rotator cuff in the shoulder is torn. She also has two herniated disks at lumbars 5 and 6. Her head was struck hard, which is the reason for the memory loss because the left central part of the brain suffered damage. We've also noted a significant hearing loss in the left ear. We are anticipating significant nerve damage in both legs. You will also notice superficial burns and cuts to her face and wrists due to the airbag deployment."

"Is she going to make it?" he asked.

"Yes, I believe she will, but like we have said, the next forty-eight hours will be crucial. We need for her vitals to stabilize and her white blood cell count to come down. These would be signs she is heading in the right direction. I will check back on her before my shift is done. Is there anything you need?"

"Who? Me? Oh, no. Please just fix her. She is my everything. Doc, thank you for everything you're doing for her. I will tell you one thing: Anya is a fighter. She will push through anything." He pulled out his phone and dialed Jess's number.

"So how is she doing? Any better? Do they know what happened yet?" Jess asked.

"No, not yet, but it's pretty serious. I'm worried," he replied. This was not part of the plan. They had spent months planning every step carefully to get the proof and send it to Sergeant Jackson. "I'm still in shock. None of it makes sense. The officer said she never saw it coming. There was a man at the scene, and he said the other car, a Honda Accord, just sped up and crossed the double yellows as if they were trying to hit her car!"

"Why would anyone want to hurt Anya on purpose? She is sweet and kind. You're right, it does not make sense," Jess said.

TRACY ANNE BERTINI

"Someone was following us just before we got separated. I had to tell Anya to run to the truck to get the information files to Sergeant Jackson. I should never have forced her to split up. That was stupid! I was supposed to protect her, and I failed. I'll never forgive myself for that. We had been so careful up to that point. Literally one hour longer, and it would have been out of our hands. The whole thing would have unraveled. How do regular people get put into these types of situations?" he asked.

"Sometimes we will never know why we are called to do things," Jess responded. "Our biggest challenge now is to help Anya make a full recovery and get our girl back."

"OK, I'll call a few people and see about getting the ramps and equipment we need to be delivered to the house so we can bring her home as soon as she is ready. Jess, can you come by and sit with her later so I can run some of those errands?"

"Absolutely, I'll be there soon. Can I bring you anything?" she asked.

"No, I'm good for now. I just need to get her home," he answered as he hung up the phone.

CHAPTER TWENTY-THREE

WAKING UP AT home, Sebastian felt both peace and the calm before the storm all in one. He had not seen his father yet; it was late when he got in last night. "Today is a new beginning for us both, Father," he said as he stepped out of bed and walked toward the breakfast tray left in his room. He grabbed the newspaper and read the headline: LOCAL FARMER WORKING TO MAKE A DIFFERENCE AND HOW WE CAN ALL HELP. "Now that is just what I am looking for. I must go and meet this farmer." He enjoyed his breakfast on the balcony overlooking the west gardens.

After breakfast, he started his morning ritual of weights, cardio, yoga, and meditation and then finally shower and grooming. Sebastian laid out each piece of clothing on the bed methodically; shoes were placed at the bed's side to match his suit for that day. Today was important, probably one of the most important days of his life. He had waited his entire life to be able to show his father he not only was useful but also could be the son he had always pushed him to be.

Walking down the stairs, he could smell the fine Cuban cigar coming from the library. He knocked on the door and walked in. "There you are, Sebastian. How was the drive? It must have been late when you arrived. The butler was waiting for your arrival. You know I'm only going to give you one shot at this today, no second chances, so you had better bring your A game! I have arranged for the brothers to all come this evening, and you will have the floor. I hope you know that, once you go down this road, there is no turning back. It is a way of life from personal to business. It is all-consuming."

"Father, I would not have asked you if I did not think about everything. I promise I have figured out what the brothers could not. You'll be impressed!"

There was a knock at the door. "Excuse me, sir, your car has arrived. Shall I tell them you will need a few more moments?"

"No, that will not be necessary. I want nothing more than to get this day going! Father, I will see you soon. I am looking forward to the meeting." Sebastian grabbed his briefcase and headed to the car waiting outside.

"Good day, sir," the driver greeted.

"Why, yes, it is. You have no idea just how good! We are heading into the city. I have a lunch date."

"'Sounds like this is going to be your day!" the driver added. The car left the driveway and headed east on the highway.

"The restaurant is on Sixteenth Street. You can park in the parking deck around the corner."

"Absolutely, sir, we should be there in about fifteen minutes." They took the exit and headed toward Sixteenth Street. "The traffic is unusually heavy for this time of day," the driver told him.

"It is fine. We have plenty of time. Nothing will ruin my day today," Sebastian responded.

A few minutes later, they pulled into the parking deck. The driver exited and opened the door. "Sir, we have arrived. I will be waiting for you."

"Thank you. I should be done in about two hours, no longer. You could go get a coffee or grab lunch in the meantime if you'd like." He headed upstairs toward the restaurant.

Pulling open the door, he was promptly greeted with a friendly smile from the hostess. "Good afternoon, sir. How can we help you today?" she asked.

"Good afternoon to you as well. I have a reservation under Tutworth."

"Of course, Mr. Tutworth. I have your table ready, if you would follow me this way." She led him through the room and stopped at the best table there, right by the kitchen. "Mr. Tutworth, here we are, the chef's table. I honestly believe you will enjoy your experience. It is a one-of-a-kind experience that our executive chef takes a lot of pride in. He has prepared an exceptional menu for you today. Mike also shares your passion for fresh, organic, wholesome food and ingredients. His family owned and ran a farm for many years, so he grew up with the freshest locally grown food. Oh well, I'm sorry. We just love his approach to cooking and staying true to his roots. So we tend to brag on him a bit. Mr. Tutworth, may I get you a drink? Mike will be right out to go over the experience he has planned for you today."

"Thank you. I am looking forward to meeting Chef Mike and experiencing the meal with him from start to finish. I'll have a martini." Sebastian looked around the room while he waited for the chef.

A few moments later, Mike came to the table and introduced himself. "Hello, Mr. Tutworth. It is a privilege to have you dine with us today. I have prepared an amazing food experience for you. I thought we would start with a fresh yellow beet salad. I have paired the beets with a balsamic strawberry reduction and a light goat cheese topping. I really like the way the bitter plays with the sweet of the strawberries. Please enjoy. I will be back in a few moments to share the rest of today's menu with you."

"Mike, this does look fantastic. The color of the beets is superb, and it is plated and presented beautifully. I have had the privilege of dining all over the world, and this looks like it could stand with any of those dishes."

"Please enjoy." Mike waited for him to take a bite.

"Excellent burst of flavor as I expected," Sebastian responded. The lunch was off to a good start. Sebastian had spent months researching Mike and his culinary journey, as well as his personal life.

In the kitchen, the sous-chef asked, "So what do you think, Mike?"

"It's still too early to say, but he doesn't seem as hard-ass as everyone had warned. He's just a man and puts his pants on one leg at a time. Of course, those pants cost more than all our pants." He laughed as they were putting the finishing touches on the salad. "Besides, we really do make art with food. I'm confident in what we do! No worries, guys, we

TRACY ANNE BERTINI

got this." Mike was always the captain to pull everyone together and get the team fired up.

Walking back into the dining room, Mike approached the table and placed the salad down in front of Sebastian. "I really think you will enjoy this salad as well. It is all locally grown produce. I've dressed it lightly with a mixture of vanilla balsamic and Mediterranean herb olive oil. By adding the cheeses and fruit, it gives a sweet and nutty taste."

The next hour and a half went on like this. Mike would bring out the next course with an explanation of the thought put into the dish. Each recipe was handcrafted and full of love. Sebastian knew his gut feeling about Mike was spot on; he would provide the perfect cover for his plan. Mike was feeling great about how lunch was going when he took a dessert out to Sebastian as his final presentation. "Mr. Tutworth, it has been a pleasure and honor to share my vision of food with you. I am hoping I will see you again." Mike extended his hand to shake his.

Sitting back from the table, Sebastian said, "Although the food was impressive, the surroundings were lacking at best." He continued to complain while Mike stood there and listened.

How could I have misread this guy? He seemed to be enjoying himself the whole time, he thought. "Well, Mr. Tutworth, I do apologize. I had no idea you were not comfortable or not enjoying your visit with us." Mike continued to apologize.

Suddenly, Sebastian put his hand up and said, "*Stop!* Do not be sorry. You thought you delivered the best food and service, correct?"

"Yes, I did," Mike replied.

"Then why are you apologizing? You need to be confident in yourself. A man has to own whatever he is doing, selling, or promoting. Confidence is everything in this world. Now what did you really want to say to me when I started complaining?" He prompted Mike.

"What an ass! Your education may be world-class, but you, sir, do not have any! Who do you think you are?"

Sebastian smiled. "Yes, exactly! That's it. Now you've got it. I was an ass. You should've called me out on that. I knew you were perfect for this new position in my company. You have to have an open mind. It would be working with food and lack of water, stuff like that. Are you interested?" he asked while looking directly at Mike. "Take a few days to think it over. I will send a car for you in three days as this project cannot wait and must get started soon. I will answer any questions at that time. Shall we say 3:30 p.m. then?"

"I would be interested in speaking with you in more details regarding this endeavor. Sure, three thirty will work. See you then," Mike answered and started to walk away.

"Oh, Mike, the food was fantastic. I had to make sure you could take criticism. The world I live in is the land of the masters of the universe, the men and money that shape our very existence. See you in three days at three thirty."

"I will see you then. Have a nice afternoon, Mr. Tutworth, and thank you for the advice."

Back in the kitchen, the staff was waiting as they could tell from his body language that Mike was defusing a situation like always. Mike had always said, "Kill them with kindness, but at the end of the day, you can't be everything to everybody."

"So how did that go? It looked pretty intense. What was the problem? That was some of the best food I've seen you prepare."

"It was a life lesson. Long story short, be confident, and nice guys finish last sometimes." Mike shook his head. "I'm not going to change who I am. I love to make people happy, a people pleaser, I guess. 'Wonder if he'll give us a bad review on one of those sites." Everyone burst out in laughter.

"You know those sites are skewed anyway. Unless you have several reviews under your belt, they won't even post it. So of course, everyone who bitches about everything is the squeaky wheel!" the sous-chef said. "There is a special place for people like that. I'm just saying. Obviously, they are unhappy in life."

"Well, he has a proposition for me regarding a position. We are going to meet at his office in three days. We shall see. I mean, I can at least go and hear him out. There's no harm in that, right?" Mike asked.

"I think it's great. Good luck. You just never know when a door will open," said the prep cook.

CHAPTER TWENTY-FOUR

M IKE AND JOE were leaving Stacy's viewing. Getting into the vehicle, Joe noticed the black cars were still sitting there, and they had to have been there for at least two hours. "Hey, Mike, the black trucks are still parked over there."

Mike looked over slowly. "Hmm, strange. They don't look as if they have moved at all. This is your neck of the woods. Is it normal to see a group of trucks just parked for hours not near any houses?" he asked.

"No, not usually, at least not around the downtown area. There's a school zone right there. Now if this was near the woods, that's a different story, with all the hunting that happens here. Keep your eye on them while we leave. Can you get a plate number?" Joe replied.

They pulled out onto Dahlonega Highway and started northbound toward the hotel. "What time is the funeral tomorrow?" Joe asked.

"It's at nine thirty at the Lutheran church. So we haven't talked about the other reason you came here. Is everything OK?"

Joe replied, "I spoke with the attorney today. All the arrangements have been made. It's just so hard to say a final goodbye, ya know. We've tried everything. There is no hope left. She's gone."

"I don't even know what to say. I am sorry. Death would've been easier to deal with. You grieve, but you at least have closure. This is agonizing. Life-altering decisions, how do you even do it, weighing what she would've wanted versus what you want?"

Mike looked up just then and noticed the black SUV pulling beside the car; as it passed them, the driver lowered his sunglasses and stared at both of them through the driver's side window. There was a handwritten sign held in the back window that said, "We know where you are. We are watching."

"Mike, get that plate number when the asshole drives by. I have a friend on the force. He can look it up."

"Got it!" Mike quickly wrote it down on an envelope in the car.

"This world is getting crazier by the day. One more day, and we are heading to the cabin. We have to stop and get some supplies. I'll stop tonight and get everything packed. We mostly just need some meats, pantry stuff. The cabin has great gardens with tons of fresh produce. In fact, you'll be in heaven!" Joe said with a smile.

Arriving back at the hotel, they got changed and headed to the store for supplies. The grocery stores were getting emptier by the hour. Mike turned on the radio, and they heard the CDC spokesperson again giving the latest statistics about the virus. "Hey, did you hear that over one million worldwide are ill!"

"Did I hear that right?" Mike said to Joe. "Wow, that is crazy! I don't even know what to say. How many deaths have occurred from the infection?"

"I don't know. They haven't said, but weren't they saying a few days ago it was 75 percent that was dying from the illness?"

Mike was looking out the window and answered, "Yes, I think so. I can't even imagine."

"Hey, you brought the wire cutters, right? What about the flashlight?"

"I brought it all. Why, Joe? What are we doing anyway? You never said."

"We have to go get a radio. I left out here years ago to call Buzz. He wasn't comfortable talking on the phone. He said it wasn't safe. After the day we are having, I would rather err on the side of caution."

"I agree, Joe, it is weird."

"Let me call my friend at the sheriff's department quick and let him know what we are doing. It could be considered trespassing. 'Always good to have the law on your side, right?" Joe picked up his phone and dialed the number.

"OK, I know there must be something wrong if you're calling me on this line. I cringe to even ask, but how are things?" the voice on the other line asked.

"Well, they are as good as can be expected, but I'm actually calling because I'm heading over there. I'm not looking for a lecture. I need to get a couple of things. Is it still guarded heavily?" Joe asked.

"Dinnertime is the best time, when the guards make the shift change. Joe, be careful. Something is going on up there, a lot of activity going in and out of that area. I don't have as much pull as I did back in the day. The GBI and the Feds have jumped in and taken over that whole area. Get in and get out as quick as possible. Joe, if you need me, I'm here."

"Thanks. I appreciate it, more than you'll ever know. Let's hope this is the last time we will have to have any of these discussions."

"Oh, one more thing, Joe, if you get in a pinch, call the old number and ask for Bob. He can assist in whatever you need. I mean, whatever. You did not hear that from me."

Mike asked, "What was that all about? It sounded like some pretty secret stuff."

"It's just more ghosts from the past, Mike. I did not think I would ever be doing any of this again! Listen, when we get there, if you don't want to come, you can stay in the vehicle and keep watch."

"Nah, I'm in, Joe. I've got your back."

They pulled down the dirt road and saw the gate. "OK, Mike, here we go. Open the glove box and grab the two guns in there, just in case."

"Got it. Anything else we need?" Mike asked.

"Under the maps in there is a compass and two walkie-talkies. Go ahead and grab them too. No matter what happens, Mike, keep your eyes open." They both walked past the gate and toward the cement buildings in the distance, looking all around as they continued forward.

Suddenly, they heard something coming from the east near the river. "Shhhh. Mike, did you hear that? I could've sworn it was a moan or groan."

"I didn't hear anything, but I wasn't near you. I was still looking toward the buildings. I thought I saw a figure up there moving," Mike answered.

"All right, let's head to the building and get out of here!" They walked up the hill into the structure that stood on top. Joe noticed footprints heading in and up the stairs. "Mike, do you see those footprints?"

"Yes, I do. They look relatively small, definitely not a man's print."

"We go in here, up the stairs, keep to the right. I'll go first to make sure it's good. You keep your eye on the stairs." Joe started heading toward the second floor; the concrete walls were crumbling in some locations.

"Joe, what the hell is this place?" Mike asked.

"Hold on. I'll tell you all about it when we leave. Come in through this door. OK, we should see lockers on the far side of the room. If I remember correctly, it should be in locker 811. Ah, there we are, locker 811. Thank god it's still here."

"What's the combo?" Mike asked.

Joe walked over, grabbed the lock, and turned the numbers to 0217. The lock opened. "Mike, bring that duffel bag over. We have to get as much of this stuff as we can carry out of here." Joe motioned to the contents of the locker.

"What is all of this stuff?" Mike asked.

"Supplies I had placed here years ago." They filled the bag with all the items from the locker. Walking briskly back out the way they came in, Joe heard it again—that noise coming from the east. "Mike, did you hear it that time?"

"I did. What the hell is it?" Mike asked.

"Don't know. Let's walk closer that way and see if we spot anything." They walked by the embankment next to the river and saw a figure lying half in the river. "Good god, who could that be? Mike, I'll head back to the truck and grab the first aid kit. Do you want to head down there and keep your eye on them? I'll be right back."

"Sure, I'll head down now. Give me one minute." Mike slid down the Georgia clay and onto the riverbank. He walked over to the lifeless body, and he gently rolled it over and could barely make out anything. The body was covered in caked-on mud and dirt. "Hey, Joe, it's a woman. I have no idea what she was doing, but she has a nasty gash on her leg and another on her forehead. Her face is all swollen. She has a pulse. She's alive!"

"Mike, can you carry her up, or do you need help?"

"I've got her. Just meet me at the ridge."

"You got it, Mike!" Joe ran to the truck and grabbed the first aid kit and quickly ran back to the side of the hill.

"Here, Joe, can you grab her?"

"I got her. She looks like she's in bad shape. We should probably get her to the hospital," Joe responded.

Then they heard gunshots and sirens. "Mike, we have to go now! Run! They are coming!" Joe yelled as they grabbed the woman and headed toward the truck.

"I'll lay her in the back seat, Joe. You start the truck!" Mike placed her in the back seat and jumped into the passenger's seat in front with Joe.

"Let's go! We are out of here!" Joe quickly drove off, speeding down the road. "Mike, can you see anything? Are they following?" Joe asked.

"I can't see anything right now. Just keep driving."

CHAPTER TWENTY-FIVE

SEBASTIAN WAS ELATED with the possibilities of how tonight would go. He had planned everything to a tee. He dressed in his best suit and headed toward the library to join the meeting. Knocking on the door, he heard his father's voice. "Enter, Sebastian." He walked through the doors and headed toward the table where eleven men sat waiting. "Sebastian, you should know everyone at the table, I believe."

"Good evening, gentlemen. It is a real honor to meet with you tonight. I am both humbled and excited. You will not regret one minute of our meeting this evening. Please have a seat as I would like to proceed." Sebastian motioned to the table, and the men began to sit down.

"Well, before we get started, Sebastian, I want to remind that anything you hear or see is not to leave these walls. We have worked for many years to stay under the radar, so to speak, to carry out our mission in secrecy. We do not showboat with the power that has been bestowed on us. We also have all vowed to make the mission the first thing in all our lives, even willing to die for our case if need be. You do understand this, son? Right?" There it was—the first time Johnathon called him a son and meant it, not as part of an insult but as a father sharing a significant milestone in his son's life.

"Father, in front of you, your peers, and my God, I swear my undying allegiance to this group of men. Now if I could, before we get started, just tell you what I have come up."

The man in charge said, "Sebastian, there is plenty of time for that after. Your father has told us all about your artificial rain project and how you have planned to implement within the local farms. You are all set to start? This is correct information, yes?"

"Yes, sir, it is. We are ready to implement my plan as soon as you are ready. I made my final preparations today and met with a bright young chef. He was raised on a farm and has made it his life's passion to grow and use organic, non-GMO foods. He also is quite familiar with the local citizens, so we will have no problems getting everything in place."

"Then I say welcome, and let's get him inducted tonight!" The men walked over to the other table and started the robe ritual.

"Sebastian, you are now not only my son but also my brother. I am proud of you, son. This is a fantastic opportunity for you, and I cannot wait for everything to reveal itself." His father beamed from ear to ear. The pride Sebastian felt at that moment was everything he had always wanted and then some. He was finally accepted by his father.

"Here is your robe. Watch and do exactly what we do." The hooded man handed the robe to him. Sebastian followed each step meticulously. Each man then grabbed a white candle, got in a line, and headed to the bookcase. He could remember each step like it was yesterday. "Down the stairs and through the hall to the great room with the altar. Then we will all kneel." He walked through each step in his mind as he did many times over the years. It was finally time.

"Sebastian, we bestow the great honor of joining us. We have been the protectors of truth and enlightenment for many years, starting with our forefathers. You now are also part of a higher calling. With the power that we have been given, at this moment, I welcome you to the brotherhood. No longer are you in the dark that society would keep you. You, Brother Sebastian, are now in the light of knowledge. There is no turning back from your destiny. You are one with the light and infinite. We have traveled through time and space to find our rightful place in the universe." Standing there in the presence of these powerful men made him feel almost invincible. This was the moment he had waited for his whole life.

As they approached the altar, he noticed a young woman again sitting there, and he knew it was time for the blood sacrifice. He often wondered what happened to the young lady years ago. The hooded man handed Sebastian the jeweled goblet and said, "Brother Sebastian, you will catch the blood of our sacrifice and gift to the infinite. This is an honor, and we would like for you to take this first step with us tonight. Sebastian, will you accept this honor?"

He answered, "I will with every fiber of my being here and in the afterlife." He held the goblet as the hooded man once again slid the sharp blade over the woman's wrists, and the crimson blood ran into the cup. Each cut was exact in size and location. The whole experience was surreal for Sebastian as he had never been accepted into any type of group; he was always outside looking in.

Step by step, they continued through the ritual with chanting. Another brother approached Sebastian and handed him a scroll with the ancient chants on it. "Brother, this is a gift from the infinite. Guard it with your life." He bowed in front of Sebastian and walked away. One by one, the men walked toward him, bestowing on him ancient gifts of enlightenment.

"Now, Brother Sebastian, please carry her to the altar and place her in the center of the circle. Be ever so gentle as she has now been purified and is the property of the infinite." He laid her gently down in the circle, brushed her hair from her face, and arranged it as if she had just stepped out of a salon. She was beautiful and looked almost angelic lying there somewhere between life and death. "We must take her to the edge of *mortality* to purify her soul and make her a worthy gift. It must always be our gift's choice. They have to volunteer to be purified. You must never take them against their will. You can never speak of what you see or hear in our sacred circle."

The hooded man then took the blade and carved the symbol into her chest. The wound only bled for a brief moment as it was superficial. The woman was in a trancelike state and apparently felt no pain. They passed around the cup, and each took a sip. The man in the hooded robe then looked at the group and said, "This, my brothers, is the blood of life. Drink, and you will be one with the infinite. We welcome Brother Sebastian into the light with us. Now it is time to carry out the plan of the infinite. With our new brother, we will move forward." He turned to Sebastian and held out his hand. "Please join me on the quest as

TRACY ANNE BERTINI

we take back the balance in nature. The fools who have not found enlightenment will now pay with their lives! The infinite demands that the balance be restored, and only the pure, enlightened souls will enter into the new world with our brothers and sisters. We will make this world a reality, for now is the time!"

They all began to chant again in Latin. After the ritual, the leaders all met in the library once again. "Sebastian, join us at the table and claim your rightful place among us." His father pointed to the table.

"Gentlemen, I am honored to be one with all of you," he humbly said.

"Please tell us your plan now, Sebastian, the one your father has told me you were working on."

"Of course, I am excited to let you all in on my part of the plan. As you know, I have continued my father's work, and I have made tremendous breakthroughs."

"Yes, tell us now. We are ready, brother." The men were elated with the thought that it was finally time.

CHAPTER TWENTY-SIX

ANYA LAY IN the back of the truck as they sped down the road. She was still unconscious. "Mike, how is she doing?" Joe asked.

"She's still breathing, but she's not moving much."

"Well, we are just going to head to my friend's house. He's a physician. He can care for her." Just then, Joe's phone rang. "Hello? Hey, Jeff, how are you doing?"

"Not so great, Joe. I miss her so much!" Jeff replied. "Listen, we've decided that, with all the virus stuff, we are just going to have a small burial and forego the funeral. Stacy would've wanted everyone to stay safe. They are asking everyone to stay home now. Have you seen the news?"

"No, I haven't heard anything. OK, Jeff, we are going to head to the cabin, and then if you want, you can come up and ride this out with us after the funeral."

"Thanks, but I'm going to stay with her family for a while. Hey, thanks for everything, you guys coming all the way here with me. It means a lot. Sorry you're stuck here now to wait this out."

"We wouldn't have been anywhere else. Stacy was important to us both."

"Hey, let me know when you guys get to the cabin."

"OK, Jeff, we will. Talk to you soon, buddy."

"What was that all about?" Mike asked.

"This virus is getting out of control. They are going to do a private funeral. I guess they are closing state offices and asking people to limit their exposure to the public."

"So we're just going to head to the cabin then? What about her?" Mike looked at the woman in the back seat.

"I guess we will take her with us. If they are closing things down, we may not be able to get her help. I have some basic medical supplies at the cabin."

Just then, Mike noticed the black SUVs slowly following them. "Hey, Joe, I think we have company."

"Yeah, I saw them a quarter of a mile back. We still have about an hour drive, so let's keep our eye on them and see what they are up to."

"You got it!" Mike said.

As they made their way up toward the mountains, Joe decided to stay on the back roads; it was easier to lose whoever was following them. "Joe, they are gaining on us."

"All right, hold on. We are going to get rid of them." Joe sped up and maneuvered the curves in the mountain roads, but they stayed right behind them.

"Don't lose them, you idiot! They have her in the car. We need to get her! The boss will not tolerate another mess-up!" They pulled up along the side of the vehicle, rolled down the window, and fired.

"Holy shit! Who the hell are these people?" Mike asked as he grabbed the gun from the bag. He stuck it out the window and returned fire. The bullets were flying back and forth from each vehicle.

"Mike, I'm going to slam on the brakes and then head right. Get the tires! On three. Ready?"

"Yes!" Mike steadied the shot.

"One, two, three!" All at once, the vehicle came to an abrupt stop; while the tires smoked, Mike shot out the two tires on the driver's side of the SUV. The truck swerved and pulled over.

"All right, they pulled off the road. Let's get out of here!" Mike said to Joe as the vehicle sped off and headed north on Highway 400.

"Sir, they got away. I understand, but they had a gun as well. No, you are correct. It is not an excuse. I'm just letting you know the circumstances. They headed toward Highway 400. I can have another car here in ten minutes."

The voice on the other end simply said, "I will handle it from here. You have failed me for the last time. I will not forget this lack of dedication!"

"Sir, I apologize. Sir?" The phone call had ended.

"Mike, keep your eye out for anybody else. We need to call Buzz on the two-way as soon as we are safely away from them." Joe picked up his phone and dialed a number. "Hey, it's me. Listen, we will be coming in hot. I think we lost our tail, but you know how they are. I believe that it's the same people."

The woman on the other end said, "It is! That is what I was going to tell. I'll set everything up but be careful. It's not safe. We should be there in about twenty minutes."

"Thanks!" Joe hung up the phone and turned toward Mike. "You don't see them, right? How is she doing?"

Mike replied, "No, I don't see any sign of them. She is still in and out but still breathing."

They followed the rest of the winding roads to the cabin deep in the woods. "OK, Mike, we are here. We have to get this radio set up and call Buzz. Let's get her inside and upstairs to one of the rooms and let her rest while we check in with Buzz."

"I'll bring her upstairs, and I have to call Sebastian and let him know I will be waiting it out from here. You go ahead and call Buzz." Mike picked up the woman covered in the dark red Georgia clay and brought her upstairs to the bedroom. He gently laid her on the bed and grabbed a basin of water, some soap, and a facecloth and placed it on the side table next to the mirror. He figured she may want to clean some of the dirt off once she had felt better. "Hey, Joe, do we have a blood pressure cuff?" he yelled down the stairs as Joe was coming up the staircase.

"Yes, we do. Here you go. I brought up bottled water too."

"Great, I will leave it here for her."

"I'm going to get the radio going." Joe started to set up the old two-way radio on the kitchen counter. "OK, here goes nothing," he said as he turned the dial to the channel Buzz would always use. "Buzz, it's Joe. Do you copy?" The static feedback was loud but no Buzz. "Buzz?

Are you there?" Joe continued over the next fifteen minutes to call out to him.

Mike walked into the kitchen and pulled out some food for dinner; he turned on the TV and heard the following: "We are now declaring a state of emergency in all fifty states. The pandemic has now claimed over two million lives worldwide. The CDC and World Health Organization are still stumped on how to control this virus. It seems to be taking on a life of its own." They were showing pictures from all over the world—sick people, businesses closed, cars abandoned, empty grocery shelves. "The looting has now started, and the violence is getting out of control. It is a chapter straight out the book of Revelation. Could this finally be it? Will this wipe out the human race? We will continue to broadcast as long as we can with the information we are getting. We have quarantined in place at the station to avoid contact with the virus."

"Joe, you have to see this!" Mike yelled up to him.

"All right, I'll try Buzz in a little bit. I'll be right down." Joe walked past the room where the woman slept; he peeked in and felt like he knew her but had no idea how. He shook it off and chalked it up to the day they had escaping from the men in black. Joe joined Mike in the kitchen. "So what is going on?" he asked.

CHAPTER TWENTY-SEVEN

PANDEMIC! NO ONE IS SAFE. THINGS YOU NEED TO KNOW TO LIVE THROUGH THIS APOCALYPTIC PLAGUE! "Well, well, well, interesting. It seems they have no idea what is going on. Fools! Running around like sheep. This is going to be easier than I could've ever imagined." Sebastian was reading the local newspaper headline as he enjoyed his morning coffee. He took pride in his part in all of this. The brothers were right: it had come, and he was a key player. None of this was possible without his help. "I can feel the power running through my very essence. It is getting stronger. It is time for the next step. I must go to the Guidestones and initiate the next step."

Everything had aligned perfectly—the stars, his plan, and the pandemic. He thought back to that night when he had been enlightened. He had explained his master plan to the brothers. He would control the world population and bring perfect balance to nature. It appeared the plan was going according to schedule. Sebastian had been working exclusively on that end of the project. While in college, his father sent him an old notebook that contained many formulas; at the time, he had no idea what they were for, but now he was enlightened and knew what had to be done to restore the natural balance.

His phone began to ring. "Hello?"

"Sebastian?" the voice on the other end had asked.

"Yes, this is Sebastian. Who, may I ask, is this?"

"It's me. I mean, it's Charlotte. Sebastian, are you there?" she asked.

"I am. How are you, Charlotte? I figured when I hadn't heard back from you after my message, I wasn't going to. It has been years. Did you finish school?"

"I did, and I heard you graduated a few years ago, top of your class! I'm so proud of you! I called your office, and they said you were in Georgia on personal business. Is that so?"

"Yes, it's true. I am in Georgia, attending a funeral, but it seems as though it has been canceled because of the pandemic."

"Oh, Sebastian, it is so scary, isn't it? So many people dying for no logical reason. I would like to speak to you if we could, please."

"I do have some time over the next few days. I'm heading toward South Carolina tomorrow but must make a brief stop in Elberton."

"What is in Elberton? I thought there were just that granite company and farmlands."

"Don't you worry about what's in Elberton." He playfully laughed. "You never have to worry, Charlotte."

"I can be in Charleston by the following morning. Shall we meet for brunch?"

"Yes, that would be lovely."

"Sebastian, I look forward to your visit. I'll see you in a couple of days."

"Charlotte, I am pleased you called. In fact, your timing is almost impeccable. I am not the boy you remember! I will count the days."

"Good night, Sebastian." Charlotte hung up the phone and headed to her room. "What did he mean by he's not the boy he was? Obviously, he was a man now." She shook her head and closed the shades.

"Hmm, my Charlotte, why now? I have been willing this for a lifetime. Could this be the last piece of the puzzle?" Every little thing was moving into place for him to take his rightful seat and lead the brothers into the dawn of illumination.

He walked to the terrace and sat down, staring up at the star-filled sky. He pulled out the notebook from his father and opened to a creased page that had a passage he had read over and over through the years. Sebastian always felt connected to the passage on another level. He sat for a while more and then went back into the room, packed his bag, and laid out his clothes for his trip. Then he pulled out his briefcase and checked to make sure the contents were perfect. He needed to be in Elberton to prepare and set up to take his rightful throne. The anticipation ran through his blood, and the sheer excitement of the day was almost overwhelming for him.

The two-way radio started to go off. Joe ran up the stairs. "Buzz, is that you?"

"It is. I'm at the airport now. Look, it's worse than I thought."

"Have you seen the quarantine process?" Joe asked.

"I have. Almost 111,000 people were sent down to the areas. Listen, we are going to head down there. The shift change will occur in a few hours, and we will have time to slip in and act like one of them. If you don't hear from us by tomorrow night, send help. You remember my buddy Steve, right?"

"Yeah, Steve, I do," Joe answered.

"OK, well, call him if you don't hear from me. He will know what to do and where to find me. Listen, Joe, you need to be careful too."

"All right, Buzz, I actually agree with you this time. We were leaving the viewing for Stacy, and a black SUV sped out and followed us and then started shooting at the car. Mike shot out the tires and stopped them from following us, so we headed straight to the cabin. Hey, Buzz, you need to know. When I was there at the airport down in quarantine, I was in building 5, but I heard them mention building 3, and it didn't sound good at all. You don't want to act sick. Everyone who was down there wasn't actually sick. It was some roll call of sorts. I haven't even had time to really put thought into it. There is a woman with three little children. Her husband is a soldier. Find her. She has great instincts, and her kids were scared."

"Joe, you have plenty of firepower, right? I have a feeling it's going to be a bumpy ride."

"OK, Buzz, be careful, and I'll wait to hear from you tomorrow. Good luck, buddy."

"Joe, watch out for men in black. They are always watching and listening. You know we like to have fun and joke, but this is no joke!"

Joe headed back to the kitchen, where Mike was finishing dishing up dinner for the three of them. "Do you want me to bring this up to her?" Mike asked.

"No, it's OK. I will after we eat. She was still sleeping when I walked by after talking to Buzz."

"What did old Buzz have to say?"

"He was heading to the airport tonight to see what is going on. Hey, Mike, what do you know about the murals that are painted in the Denver Airport?"

"Hmm, well, fact or urban legend?" he said and laughed out loud. "OK, the facts I know are a Chicano artist painted four murals originally. Two have since been painted over because they were offensive. The first is what some say a depiction of the end of the world, a general of some sort with a machete in one hand piercing through a dove, which is a universal sign of peace. Then in the other hand is an assault rifle. The general also is wearing a gas mask and standing in front of what looks like bombed-out buildings. If that wasn't weird enough, it gets even weirder. So there are these waves or ripples emanating from him, almost eluding a chemical poison or some kind of mass genocide. Then on the left, there is a long line of women holding their dead babies. In the bottom right, some sort of document looks as if it were falling through the air. There are also a few children who either look dead or are sleeping on a pile of bricks.

"The next one is also unnerving as it appears to be a mass funeral. There are three distinct coffin-looking rectangles across the bottom, and each one has a female in it who has passed. Each of them is represented in their native attire, holding flowers or gifts in their crossed hands. One looks to be Native American, one looks African, and the girl looks German. If you look closer at the girl, she is holding a Bible and a pocket watch, maybe to symbolize time ran out. A large leopard is also dead across the top of the coffins, and there are many flowers in the middle. Then there are five other people looking on in sadness or horror at the scene. There are actually a few animals that look sad at the scene as well. Then there is a girl reading a paper map or instructions to something. An older woman is actually taking animal species and putting a glass display-type box over them to protect them from what is in the distance, I assume. The trees are all ablaze, and in the far-off distance, you can see a city of some sort, but it is way off.

"The third is a very vibrantly colored mural except for the bottom right, where it appears the general is now dead. He is lying clutching his rifle. There are doves standing on his lifeless body. There are children from all parts of the world dressed in their traditional heritage clothing, and many of them are holding what appears to be the weapons that may have been used in war. The children are bringing them to a boy who is contorting them into something else. There are smiles on their faces and banners saying 'peace.' This one has an entirely different feel to it, like good triumphed evil. At the very bottom, the words 'war,' 'violence,' and 'hate' appear on a decaying-type stone.

"The fourth and final mural is a glance at the new world postapocalypse, I guess. It shows everyone—man, woman, and child— all coming together and surrounding a boy who has a halo-looking headdress and is growing or awakening a beautiful flower as if to say life has blossomed again. The people are from all over and are overjoyed by this boy and what he is doing. The flowers are blooming, and in the background, it has a representation of all four corners of the earth. I'm not sure if it's a reference to Jesus or a savior of some sort. There is singing and dancing, and at the bottom, it says, 'In peace and harmony with nature,' a perfect balanced world with nature."

"Wow, that is pretty crazy stuff. 'Sounds like something you would see in a movie. Who actually built the airport?" Joe asked as he headed back to the fridge and handed Mike another beer.

"Well, that's part of the weirdness as well. There is a dedication stone outside that says it was built by the New Order Airport Commission. There was never any such organization, and it has a time capsule buried under the stone to be opened in 2094. They were over budget and sixteen months behind schedule. The airport has thirty-five thousand acres, but for what, no one knows. Then smack-dab in the middle of the stone is the symbol for the Freemasons. I mean, I'm not a conspiracy theorist. I leave that to old Buzz. When you put all four of them together, it is pretty convincing, though, don't you say?"

"Are you serious? That is so crazy. I have heard about the New World Order and different societies that are trying to pick up where Hitler left off." Joe was still trying to wrap his mind around everything he just heard. "Mike, what is the story regarding the blue bronco at the entrance to the airport?"

"Oh, you mean Blucifer? That is another strange and eerie story. The artist who was commissioned to sculpt the statue was at the airport to assemble it. The size of the statue was immense and required assembly on site. He was guiding the head onto the horse, and it fell on him and crushed him. I don't know if you've ever noticed, but no matter what time of day or night it is, the eyes glow red. The local legend is that there needed to be a blood sacrifice to release the full power from the statue. So when the artist's blood was literally pooling at the base of Blucifer, people believed that it was the blood sacrifice. Now the prophecy could and would come true. This thought process was significant with the secret societies and occults."

CHAPTER TWENTY-EIGHT

"OK, YOU TAKE the rear, and I'll provide cover on three. One, two, and three!" The door to the maintenance hall swung open, and Buzz ran in first. "Keep to the side walls. Be ready for anything." The passageway was dark and had a musty smell.

The TSA officer looked over at Buzz and said, "All right, we don't have much time, so let's see what we find and go from there."

"It's the plan." They continued down the dark hall, coming to many empty doorways and airway ducts. "How much farther till we get to the back elevator that will get out us down the buildings?" Buzz asked.

"Well, we are about halfway to the tornado shelter area. That has a secret entrance to the elevator hall. Once we go through the storm shelter room, we will be entering the first in a series of small concrete block rooms. It has been relatively quiet in this part of the airport. Only a few real airport employees were coming and usually going, the maintenance men checking air quality and that sort of thing."

"We are heading down the employee elevators, right?" Buzz wanted to get in and out as unnoticed as possible. This was just a trip in to see what was going on so they could plan their next step once they were able to figure all of this out.

"Yes, if we were to try to go on the main freight elevators, the security lights would come on, and the noise they would make would literally let everyone know we are coming."

Opening the door to the shelter, they walked into the cold, dark room. Scanning the room, they noticed there were very few supplies; in fact, all that they saw were a few hazmat uniforms. "This is strange. Usually, there is food, water, and medical supplies filling up these shelves."

"Well, there is nothing that has been normal lately. Let's move on." Buzz was ready to get some answers. The elevators were straight ahead. They couldn't help but notice fifty-five-gallon barrels with the poison placard on each of them lining the hall on both sides. "Hold up!" Buzz said as he stopped and took out his phone to add this to his evidence. Shining his flashlight down the hall, the realization of just how bad this looked set in. "Shit, there must be enough here to kill off a few cities. What the hell would the airport need poison for? Is there any other paperwork or signage stating what is inside of them?"

"Man, I don't see anything, just the placard." The TSA officer continued to look over the barrels. "Well, we have to head down to the buildings and look around." The elevator headed down to the bottom floor; they could feel the air temperature change as they went deeper underground. Finally, the elevator came to a stop. They drew their guns and waited for the doors to open. What would they be met with on the other side? The adrenaline started to rush through their veins.

Buzz looked over and said, "All right, guy, we got this. No matter what happens, we stick together in and out." The doors opened, but there was no surprise; it was another long dark concrete hall. It was quiet with very dim lights, like the emergency lights after a power outage. As they made their way down the corridor, they would pause only long enough to look into a doorway and make sure no one was in these rooms. Each small concrete room resembled a cell. Each had a concrete slab that appeared to be a bed, a small toilet in the corner, and a sink. There were no windows, not even an overhead light. The hall was lined with these strange cell rooms.

"What the hell would the airport need places like this for?" Buzz asked.

"I have no idea, these doors are usually closed. I've only been down here once or twice, and I've never been inside the rooms. I just assumed it was storage or electrical and maintenance closets."

Just then, they saw a far-off dim light coming from the last cell in the hall. "OK, do you see that?" Buzz looked back and asked.

"Yes, I do, looks to be the last cell in the row on the left. Wait, do you hear that, Buzz?" They could hear a very muted moan coming from the cell.

"We need to be careful, no idea what it could be. Ready?" The TSA officer nodded yes and then headed down the hall and stopped right outside the chamber. "OK, cover me. I'm going in." Buzz said and started to glance around the corner into the small room. His eyes just stared; he could not believe what he was seeing. "Whoa, you need to come see this. You will not believe it." Buzz turned toward his partner.

The TSA officer quickly came and joined him in the doorway. "Who could do this? It's just not right." The room had one small lamp. In the corner sat two small children taking their last breaths; they were emaciated and could barely hold their heads up. They were huddled and hugging a dead woman's body. On the other side of the room, there were scratches up and down the wall; it looked like someone was trying to dig their way out of this hell using their fingernails. They entered the room and headed over to the children, but they were too late. The children died right there, holding their mother tightly. The smell of death was thick and heavy in the air.

Buzz choked on the stench and walked back out to the hall for a moment. "Are you all right, Buzz?"

"I am. I just need a moment." They decided to continue to the next group of cells. They turned the corner and were overwhelmed as hundreds of bodies lay in piles. Buzz continued to lead the way, looking into each cell as the smell continued to get worse. As they reached the end of this hall, they came to an open room with bunks. Again, there were wall-to-wall dead bodies. "What kind of hell is this?" Buzz asked. "For the love of god, who or what did this!"

On the far end of the bunk room, they saw a table with a large book and laptop on it. "Hey, I'm going to head over to the table and check it out." Buzz walked over to the table and opened the book. It had hundreds of thousands of names, dates of birth, and ages. The laptop had a shattered screen, so there was no information there.

The TSA officer was looking at some of the bodies and noticed a strange bar code tattoo on the left wrist of the dead. "Hey, Buzz, you need to see this. These bodies have a bar code on their wrists."

"A what? Did you say bar code?" Buzz looked confused as he made his way over to him. Buzz pulled out his phone again and took several photos of the bodies, not including their faces out of respect. He was also getting as many pictures of the bar codes as possible; each one was very distinct. No two were alike. The bodies were all thin with dark circles under their eyes, which were sunken in, and cheekbones were almost piercing their skin; their heads had been shaved, and all appeared to have been wearing the same clothing. "This place is literally hell on earth. May these souls be free to go to the light and continue their journey."

Buzz couldn't help but think of Pastor Thompson at a time like this. What words of encouragement would he offer up? How would you even reconcile something like this in your own mind? It shook you to the core of your soul. "As a race, humans can be so cruel and heartless against one another. Power and money are gods to way too many. Brother against brother, father against son, men against women—this is what war looks like. It makes me sick." Buzz had seen many things in his life to make him lose his faith in his God, his fellow man, and himself. He had often been angry and blamed others for things he had done. *How could God allow these crimes to happen?* He would often feed off the anger deep inside.

"This needs to be stopped. Someone needs to pay for this!" Buzz went back to the table, grabbed the book, and looked around. He noticed a sign on the wall that said "building 3." "Wow, this was the building Joe was talking about. Wait till he hears this. He's never going to believe it."

"Buzz, come on, man, stay focused. We have to get out of here and move on. We still have no idea what is causing all of this! We have to get to the bottom of this. Life as we know it depends on it."

"You're right, let's go." They left the large room and followed the signs that led to buildings 4 and 5. The arrow pointed to the right. They carefully started down that hall and noticed a weird smell, not death but an almond smell.

"Buzz, do you smell almonds? I know that sounds weird, but I swear I smell them."

Buzz took a deep breath in. "You know what, I smell it too."

"What a random smell to be down here, but it is better than the smell of death."

"Come on, man, have some respect. They are someone's families," Buzz quickly scolded.

"I didn't mean any disrespect. You know that. I am just trying to keep things lighthearted. I tend to use humor as my defense mechanism."

"I know, let's head through that hall over there. It looks like the passage gets much wider." Buzz led the way. As they entered the large oval passage, big bright lights came on overhead one by one.

"What is that? Did you touch something?"

"No way!" Buzz shouted out. They were both looking around frantically to see what was going on. Buzz looked up the ceiling of the passage and noticed large sprinkler heads. "Hey, man, look at the ceiling." He pointed to the sprinklers. "What are those used for? I don't see why you would need sprinklers like that down here in an airtight concrete cylinder. 'Seems rather odd and a bit of overkill."

The TSA officer replied, "I've never noticed those before. It does seem a bit much." As they walked to the end, they saw a window into a room with a large control panel, cameras, at least twenty-five monitors on the back wall, and a table with chairs. "Buzz, are you seeing this? Look on those screens."

On the monitors they were live feeds of different rooms. There were groups; one was a group of cells or small rooms with the dead bodies and some living people who were almost in a zombielike state. That cluster said "building 3." The next group was recording building 5, where there were many people hanging out in groups; overall, they seemed healthy. The group labeled "building 4" showed hospital beds by the hundreds and patients all hooked up to IV poles. The building 2 cluster was waiting in these strange rooms with just a chair in it; the people were lining the walls all around the chambers. The group that read "building 1" had many people being shaved, lining up, walking through various lines, and heading toward the hall they were standing in.

CHAPTER TWENTY-NINE

S EBASTIAN ARRIVED AT the hotel for his lunch; flowers in hand, he entered the dining room. "Good afternoon, sir. How may I help you today?" the host asked.

"I have a reservation for Tutworth. Is my dinner companion here yet?"

"I haven't seen them yet. Would you care to wait at the bar Mr. Tutworth?"

"Sure, I will. Thank you."

The host walked him over to the bar. "I'll let you know when your party arrives." Sebastian took a seat at the bar and ordered a drink.

About fifteen minutes later, a beautiful young woman with long blond hair neatly pulled up in a loose bun with a few curls flowing down her cheeks entered the room. Her eyes were like two dark blue pools in the ocean. She was dressed like a southern belle in her china blue dress and white cardigan. "Charlotte, look at you!"

"Wow, Sebastian, I can't believe how tall you are! About six feet three inches would be my guess." She extended her arms to embrace him.

Sebastian grabbed her back and held her for a few moments. "How long has it been, Charlotte? You are even more beautiful than I remember. Let's go sit. Our table is ready and waiting. I can't wait to hear all about the last few years and where they have taken, Charlotte."

"I am looking forward to it. I have missed you. You stopped writing to me. I thought it was two years ago. Does that sound about right?"

"Yes, that would be about right. I have been extremely busy with work and traveling for my job. I've visited the most interesting and beautiful places all over the world. You would love some of the places. We should plan to take a trip. I would love to show you the world."

"Wow, that would be an honor. I have always wanted to travel to other countries, but with taking care of Mom and Daddy, it has been impossible."

"Why? What is wrong with them, Charlotte?"

"Daddy had a stroke a few years back, and his care is too much for Mom nowadays. She just doesn't have the strength or patience to meet all his needs. It is a full-time job, to say the least, but then without Daddy's income, she had to return to work to support the household. They have always been so strong. It breaks my heart to see them going through all of this."

"Why didn't you call or write, Charlotte? You know I could've and most definitely would have helped. I will arrange for nursing staff to care for your father, and your mother can work for me from her home. I'll have the IT department set her up from a home office so she can still monitor all your father's care while she works."

"Oh no, you don't have to do that. I didn't call to get you to help us. I called mostly because I wanted to know how you were doing, and I missed your letters. They would always brighten my day!"

"I won't have another word of it, Charlotte. I will arrange everything for your family as a thank-you for your kindness to me growing up. You know the difficulties I faced, yet you were always there cheering me on with words of encouragement."

"Sebastian, you did not deserve that type of treatment from anyone, especially your father."

"I understand my father's motives now. He wanted me to reach my full potential and excel in everything I did. He instilled a work ethic in me that has served me well in the business world. His father groomed him the same way. I believe it is just the Tutworth way."

"I always wanted to steal you, run away back to South Carolina, and let Mom and Daddy raise you. Being only eight years apart, I considered you to be more of a friend than a boy I babysat. We would have such great conversations about the world and our dreams. You were so kind to me always."

"I don't know if you were aware, but I had quite the crush on you back then, the older woman!" He laughed.

"You did? I honestly had no idea," she said as she blushed and took a sip of her water. The waiter came over to take their brunch order.

"Ladies first." He was always the gentleman.

"Why, thank you, kind sir." She turned to the waiter. "I will have the eggs Benedict please."

"Excellent choice. I will have the same please. Also, can we get the lovely lady a mimosa?"

"Right away, Mr. Tutworth."

"So, Charlotte, tell me, is there a man around?"

"Oh, no, I wish, but I have yet to meet the right man. I have faith he is out there. I guess the timing is just not right yet."

"You know, Charlotte, I think we could make each other very happy. I could provide stability and comfort to your family. In return, I would have a beautiful wife to show off to the world. Let me spoil you and show you things you would never have had the opportunity to do and see. I know you do not love me, but you could grow to love me. I'm sure of it. With all my money and assets, a woman looks at me like a meal ticket. I want someone who will add to my life and whom I can trust with all my prized possessions and confide my secrets in. Think about it. I will be back in a few days after I wrap up some business in Georgia. I know this is not romantic at all, but it is one hell of a business proposition that will financially take care of your parents and you for the rest of your lives. Some of the best deals made are in the boardroom and not made out of love or passion. Keeping the emotions out of it, let us negotiate our interests. Tell me that's a deal you can't deny." Charlotte sat quietly for a moment and then looked out the window for a few more. "Charlotte? Maybe that was too forward. I do apologize. I meant no disrespect. Please, I would never want to."

"Sebastian, stop, please. I am flattered. Really, I am. I know it is coming from the best place. I was just caught off guard. I was never expecting you to say that. I don't need a couple of days. Go ahead and ask properly."

Sebastian said, "I will be right back. Please excuse me for a brief moment."

"Absolutely. I will be waiting right here."

He walked over to the manager and had a quick conversation. "So we are all set then?"

"Yes, sir. I will handle it right now! Give us about twenty minutes, and we will be all set on the terrace."

"Perfect. Thank you for your help with this."

On the way back over to the table, Sebastian couldn't help but notice the sun shining on Charlotte. She looked like an angel sitting there, and she was about to change her life forever. He walked over and asked, "Charlotte, will you please accompany me to the terrace?"

"Yes, I will."

They walked outside onto the patio and were greeted with the most beautiful music. "Welcome, Ms. Charlotte. Please follow me." They were escorted to the garden area, where there was a single table adorned with fresh flowers and lace. Harpists were playing.

"Oh, Sebastian, it is beautiful! How did you pull this off so fast?"

"I can make anything happen. I told you I will make all your dreams come true. I promise!" Sebastian proceeded to kneel on one knee, take her hand in his, and say, "Charlotte Marie, will you do me the honor of becoming Mrs. Tutworth? I promise to protect you, give you everything you could ever want or need. I vow to give you the world and put your needs before mine."

"Sebastian, I would be honored to be Mrs. Tutworth."

TRACY ANNE BERTINI

CHAPTER THIRTY

"I HAD NO idea about any of that. I'll bring the food up to our guest." Joe grabbed the plate and a glass of water. Walking up the stairs, he was thinking about his wife again; this place brought back so many memories. They had spent so much time here together. Joe hadn't been in the cabin for years. He walked into the room and set the plate on the side table. He was going to check on her wound on her face, but she had rolled onto her stomach, and he didn't want to disturb her. She was sleeping peacefully. He walked over and closed the shades. The room was dark and quiet; he walked to the bathroom and plugged in the night-light.

Back in the kitchen, Mike had opened his journal and was reviewing notes from the week's lab logs. He couldn't help but notice a few changes in the food about three weeks ago. Why didn't he see them before?

"Hey, Joe, come here for a minute. I want you to check this out and see if I'm just seeing things."

"What's up?" Joe walked over toward the table and sat.

"Well, if you look at my notes from three weeks ago, you can see the texture and color notes from the samples of food I was logging. Then all of a sudden, by the next week, the color and texture had a slight variation, but no one noted the change. You can clearly see it from the log photos. This is a problem as we are directed to note all changes, big or small. I don't recognize these initials from this entry, though. Sebastian will not be happy with this. I don't know how this could have been missed."

"Mike, you said three weeks ago roughly? That's when you were missing for ten days. You don't think it's all connected, do you?"

"Wow, I didn't even think of that. I have no idea. I just consider it incredibly weird with the timing of it and the initials I've never seen before."

"Why don't you e-mail Sebastian and see if he recognizes the initials? Maybe they had someone fill in for you while you were resting."

"That would be unlikely as it has been under pretty tight security because of the FDA and USDA approvals. Sebastian doesn't usually leave anything to chance."

"I have no idea, but it seems rather odd that, all of a sudden, there is a change while you are not there. Call Kevin. Was he there that day?"

"No, it was his regular day off."

"So you mean to tell me not one person from your usual team was there at all that day?" Joe said as he headed to the living room to put the news back on. "I don't know, man. That is all too convenient, if you ask me. Mike, you have always run such a tight ship both at the restaurant and in the lab. This feels like something else is in play."

"I agree. Something is going on. I'd rather try to get to the bottom of it before I alert Mr. Tutworth. We have security cameras in the labs. I'll ask around once we get back to Denver and see if I can figure out all of this. We got sidetracked. How is our guest upstairs?"

"She is still out. I didn't want to disturb her, so I just set the plate there, closed the blinds, and turned on the night-light. We can check her out in the morning. She seems to be OK for now. I called in a favor, and a friend is stopping by tomorrow to check her out," Joe replied.

"CDC spokesperson Ms. Hardy has just announced that the death toll has now risen to over five million worldwide and shows no signs of stopping. This virus is taking on a life of its own. The president and vice president of the United States and other top world leaders have now been relocated to top secret locations to ensure that the governments are not affected by this pandemic. Scientists are saying they have no idea how it is spreading as we have the strictest quarantine plans in place, and life as we have known it has almost come to a standstill. Besides, local mom-and-pop stores, all large chain stores, and public venues have temporarily closed up shop. The devastation is not only in the number of human casualties but also in the financial blow we are all taking from this. Will we be able to recover both as a race and financially? No one knows. We have never seen anything like this in all history. We will turn live now to Emory Hospital in Downtown Atlanta."

"Thanks, Bill. As you know, I am here at Emory, where they have been working both day and night to get any kind of breakthrough in this deadly virus's treatment. Officials are now saying they will constitute martial law and public curfew by the end of the day tomorrow. Too many people have not heeded the warning to shelter in place. This makes the task even harder for law enforcement and physicians, who are already running on fumes. One official who did not want his identity exposed did state off the record that it is odd how it does not seem too contagious in the traditional sense. None of the physicians, law enforcement, or volunteers have contracted the virus. I asked Ms. Hardy if there was any credence in his statement, and she said she could not confirm or deny those facts as they are still in a full-blown class 1 public health crisis. We will be remaining here at the hospital to keep you up-to-date with this most concerning issue. I'm Sofia reporting for the evening news. Back to you, Bill."

"Wow, thanks for the update, Sofia, and stay safe. It is absolutely amazing to me that, in this day and age, we are having so many problems in trying to get on top of this situation. Well, that's all for now. We will keep you updated as information comes in."

"Wow, what the hell is going on? I have to say, Joe, I'm glad we are up here in the mountains."

"We have made this place our own little sustainable farm. We have the chickens, pigs, a few cows, and of course the gardens with all the fruit and veggies you could want."

"Why did you go through all of that trouble? I'm just curious. It seems like a lot of work, especially if you're not even here to enjoy it," Mike asked.

"You're right. It is, but I have a few people who live here locally who continue to tend to things while I'm in Denver, and in return, they can take as much food as their families need."

"That's a neat agreement." Mike smiled and walked toward the back door. "Joe, what happened to the door back here? It looks like the lock was messed with."

"The lock? What do you mean?" Joe walked over and looked at the back door; it did look as if someone or something had messed with the lock. "I have no idea. There aren't any other houses for a few miles. Maybe just the local kids or a hiker looking for a place to rest while on the Appalachian trailhead."

"Well, I'm exhausted. It has been one hell of a day. I'm going to head upstairs and call it a night."

"All right, Mike. 'Night, man. I put your stuff in the third bedroom on the left upstairs. I'll see you in the morning."

"'Night, Joe. Oh, hey, which chicken coop are the hens in? I'm thinking having a fresh sausage frittata for breakfast." Mike really did love cooking; it was his passion. Joe was always up for a Mike original.

"Well, damn, brother, I will gladly eat that. It's the coop on the right."

Mike walked upstairs and headed down the hall. As he went by the room their guest was in, he peeked in just to make sure she was still resting peacefully. Mike also felt some strange connection or need to make sure she was OK. He was convinced it was the fact they had rescued her and been through quite the ordeal today altogether.

Joe walked out and sat on the porch swing that he and his wife would swing away on most nights as they sipped sweet tea. "I don't know if I can do this. What if I'm making a mistake? Why is this all starting again? It can't be a coincidence. I've come back to Georgia to finalize everything, and they have already found me. When will this end? I wish you were still with me. I love you more than anything." He covered his face with his hands and wept. Being stuck indefinitely was not his plan at all. Watching the fireflies and listening to the peepers was always their thing. "Oh god, I miss her! Why did this all happen? I know you give us only what we can handle, but this is too much. I can't handle it anymore." He decided to head upstairs to bed and call it a night.

CHAPTER THIRTY-ONE

"I HAVE A great idea. Let's do the ceremony for you here, sir? We can arrange everything if you'd like to," the manager had said.

Sebastian looked at Charlotte. "Well, it is not up to me. What do you think, future Mrs. Tutworth? We can wait if you'd rather. I know how close you are to your parents, and I would completely understand if you wanted them there or if you just simply want a big affair. The decision is yours!"

Charlotte paused only for a moment and said, "Let's do it!"

Sebastian answered with "Well, my soon-to-be wife, you have a lot of things to get done. I assume you have someone to help her?" he asked the manager.

"Of course. Ms. Charlotte, if you please, Mrs. Payne will take you upstairs and help you take care of everything you could ever want or need."

"Wait, Sebastian, is this weird that I used to babysit you? I don't want anyone to ever say I took advantage of the generosity of your family. Are you sure you are OK with me not being in love you? I do love you."

"Charlotte, stop. Please don't worry your pretty little head about such minor details. When have I ever cared what anyone has thought or said about me? I will make it my life's mission to make you happy, and you will fall in love with me, I promise, in due time."

"I do wish Mom and Daddy were here."

"Your wish is my command. I will see you tomorrow, and we will join our union as husband and wife. Sleep well." He kissed her on her hand and walked away. "Come now, Ms. Charlotte. We have so much to do and so little time. What kind of dress would you like to wear?"

"Dress? Oh, I haven't even given it a thought."

"No worries, child, we have plenty in the shop just a few blocks from here! We must go, no time to waste."

"Mr. Tutworth, there is a call for you at the front desk of the hotel. I'll show you the way. After you, sir."

Sebastian picked up the phone and heard a familiar voice on the other end. "Sebastian, the brothers have just arrived in Georgia. Is everything all set in Elberton?"

"Yes, Father, it is. We did have to postpone the ceremony as one of the guidelines was I needed a wife, but I am taking care of that as we speak. I will be married and head back to Georgia for the ceremony tomorrow at 3:11 p.m. This will work, right, Father?"

"We have waited for the timing to be right. I feel in the very core of my essence it is right. I will see you tomorrow and look forward to meeting the new Mrs. Tutworth. Have you told her anything?"

"No, I have not shared any of that with Charlotte. It is not necessary. She will give me the heir we need to proceed with our plan. I guarantee it."

"Great news, Sebastian. We have waited for this new dawn to come, and now it is finally here!"

Buzz continued to look into the room with the monitors. "This is much worse than we thought." He looked back and saw the door behind the TSA officer open, and a glass wall then dropped from the ceiling and separated the two of them.

"Buzz, what's going on? How did you do that?"

"I didn't. Be careful. That door behind you is opening." They both watched the hatch door open in anticipation of what was coming. Slowly, they could hear something in the distance. It sounded like crying. Just then, about five hundred people walked through the hatch; they all were shaved, and most were weak and could barely stand.

"Hey, Buzz, man, this doesn't look right. Get me out, dude." Buzz frantically looked for a knob, button, lever, some kind of mechanism or switch to open the door on this side.

TRACY ANNE BERTINI

The lights in the monitor room suddenly came on, and about eleven men entered and took their place all around the chamber. "What in the hell is going on?" Buzz ran to the corner so he would not be spotted by the men in the room. He heard the power come on to the large room and could see a red light flashing. The warning sign was also illuminated. Then he could smell almonds again.

A man's voice came over a loud speaker and started to speak. "We know you are scared. There is no need to be. Like you were told, you will be going home shortly. We just need to decontaminate you from the lies that this world has hand-fed you since the day you were born. You pray to a god who does not answer. You believe you have control in your stupid little lives when, in fact, you do not. You are weak and are sheep running around like a herd heading to slaughter. Where is your precious Messiah now? Why have you been forsaken? All of you are like insects infesting our world and using its resources blindly. If we did not stop you now, you would wreck everything. We have been chosen to be the exterminators of the vermin of society that you all are. The human race has been told time and time again to live in perfect harmony and peace with nature, but you all continue to disobey the warnings that are everywhere around you. We will extinguish your light so ours may be illuminated brighter than ever before."

Buzz sat and watched in horror as the room full of people—men, women, and children—began to sob. *Who would do this?* The air got thick, and the room felt smaller and smaller.

The TSA officer walked to the glass and yelled, "Buzz, you have to tell anyone who will listen that they have to be stopped! Buzz!" The almond smell was almost overwhelming as the crying seemed to stop almost instantly, and the bodies were left in piles on the floor as if someone's garbage. Buzz gasped and could not hold back the tears any longer. The warning lights went off, and the smell was almost gone when the door behind him finally opened. He ran out the door and up the hall; he still could not comprehend what he just saw and witnessed.

As he moved toward the exit, he was stopped by a man who seemed delirious and just kept begging for someone to help. Buzz almost knocked the man over. "I have to get out of here and get help!" By the time he reached the elevator, he was completely out of breath. The elevator could not go fast enough for him. He could now forever say he had been to hell and back.

Outside, the truck was waiting; he jumped into it and sped away. On his way toward Dillion, he noticed traffic lights were off; most of the city had gone dark. Arriving back at his bunker, he locked the door and started to call his friend Steve. "Hey, are you up?" Buzz asked.

"Yes, I am. I've been waiting for your call. So what did you find? Is it as bad as we thought?"

"Oh dear lord, it is so much worse than we could've ever imagined! Someone is literally leading the groups of passengers to their death below the airport. They are using the hidden old buildings as holding cells and death chambers. There were hundreds, no thousands, of people from all over down in that hell."

"We have to mobilize and get the people out of there. This is going to take some doing."

"I'll call Joe in the morning. Tonight we need to move on getting equipment. We need to get our hands on those transport trucks. That's obviously how they are removing the bodies from Denver International."

"OK, Buzz. I'll work on the vehicles. You work on the team. We are going to need at least forty of your top guys, no question."

"Let's get to work! The plan will be to meet at the brewery tomorrow by noon."

"God speed, my friend. Keep me posted." Steve hung up the phone, went into the closet, and pulled out his old Army Ranger duffel bag. Inside, he had a black book with all his contacts. "I really hoped I would never have to bother any of you, but it is time." He pulled out his phone and started calling.

Buzz began to restock his truck with all the supplies they would need for tomorrow's rescue mission; this was a bigger mission than he had ever planned or been part of. So many innocent lives depended on him. "Did anyone else even know this was going on?" Buzz gathered as much ammo as he could fit and then headed for the explosives. He had no idea what he would face back at Denver International.

CHAPTER THIRTY-TWO

JOE MOVED AWAY after his wife had suffered a significant brain injury during a car accident. He stayed by her side, but sadly, she never remembered him. She was never the same. Joe would try to get her to remember him and the times they had together, but nothing worked. It broke his heart to leave and go to Colorado, but there was fear in her eyes every time she would see a man whom she did not recognize near her; she would scream. He had many physicians try to explain things to her, but it didn't help. She was gone.

The divorce was just a formality, and he really did not want to go through with it. All their friends and family encouraged him to try to move forward with his life as she did not remember him. "She would not want you to not live your life because she's changed." His heart ached every day for the life they once shared. He had always promised they would renew their wedding vows when they hit twenty-five years of marriage. This was the year; he would give anything to have been planning that with her right now instead of ending it.

As he lay in bed, the sun started to peek through the shades, and he felt overwhelmed. Everything was so out of control right now. He felt alone, and he missed the smell of her perfume. He could almost swear he smelled it, but it had been years since they were at the cabin together.

Joe knew Mike would already be up and gathering eggs for breakfast. He stepped out of bed and headed to the bathroom. In the closet, his sports jerseys still hung. It was as if he still lived here and time stood still in the cabin. This would be the last time he would step foot there. He would leave it to her after the divorce. He threw on a jersey and walked out of the room down the hall.

He opened the door to the room where the woman had been sleeping. She was no longer in bed. *Where could she have gone?* "Hello? Are you OK? Are you still in here? My name is Joe, and my friend's name is Mike, and I found you in Dawson Forest yesterday. It looked like you had fallen and hit your head."

He could hear a faint voice coming from the bathroom. "I am OK. Please just give me a minute."

"OK, no problem. Are you OK? Do you need anything?" Joe leaned into the room to hear her better.

"Maybe an ibuprofen. I have quite the headache."

"Sure, I will go get one. I left you some towels on the sink in there, and there are toothbrush, shampoo, and everything that you might need."

"I think I'm OK. I just was going to get cleaned up, and I'll be out in a minute," she replied. Joe went down to the kitchen and grabbed the ibuprofen.

"Breakfast is almost ready, bud. Did you get any sleep?" Mike asked.

"A little. It's just a hard time of year for me and then being back here. It's all good. The world is just crazy right now. Hey, did you happen to see the ibuprofen? She has a headache."

"I'm sure she does. The whole right side of her face was swollen from her fall. I think I saw it in the pantry."

Joe grabbed it and headed back upstairs with fresh bottled water. He walked back to the door. "I have your pills and water. Do you want me to leave them on the table, or should I bring them in?"

"You can. You said your name was Joe, right? " she replied as she finished washing the blood off her face.

"Yes, Joe," he answered.

"Joe, food's ready! Come eat!" Mike hollered up to him.

"I'll be right there!" Joe replied. "Breakfast is ready. If you are hungry, I'll leave this on the table."

"OK, do you have a phone I can use? I need to call my friend and let her know where I am."

"Yes, there is one downstairs. You are welcome to use it."

"Thank you. I watched the news this morning. The virus is getting worse, I heard. I guess we will be stuck here for a little bit."

"Yeah, it does sound like that," Joe agreed. "I'll meet you downstairs."

Joe and Mike were sitting on the porch, eating their frittatas and joking around, trying to keep the mood light. They could hear her in the kitchen. She was getting her coffee and started to head on to the porch to join them. She walked through the door way and said, "So I know his name is Joe, and you must be Mike?"

"Yup, I am Mike! We met yesterday, but you were in and out of it. What's your name?"

"My name is . . ." Just then, Joe looked up, and they both said "Anya" at the same time. Joe's plate dropped to the ground and smashed.

"Joe, are you OK?" Mike asked as he jumped up. Joe stood there in disbelief. There she was right in front him. It had been years.

Anya turned toward Joe and said, "This is going to sound strange, but I feel like I know you."

"You do know me. We knew each other a long time ago when I lived in Georgia. How have you been? It's been forever."

"I'm doing well. My memory is a little foggy. I'm sorry. How did we know each other?"

"Well, we used to work together."

"That makes sense. Where did we work together?" she inquired.

"It was a long time ago—" he started to say.

She interrupted him and asked, "How did you guys find my cabin anyway?"

Mike looked at Joe with a shocked look on his face. "Joe, is this your—"

Joe stopped him from asking that question right now. "When we worked together, I drove you home a few times. So I remembered where the cabin was. Yesterday when we found you after your fall, you were out cold. We just wanted to make sure you got home safe. I also called Jess and told her that we were bringing you home. In fact, she should be here any minute."

"You knew Jess too?"

"Yes, quite well. I've kept in touch with her over the years."

"So you knew me before my accident then? I had a brain injury, and it caused a loss of memory. I try to joke around about it and stay positive."

"Yup, that sounds just like you, always positive!"

"It feels good to be home, and I'm glad for the company. There were men here trashing the place and looking for something a few days ago. I found a small doorway that led me under the house, and I ended up in Dawson Forest. Things have been unnerving lately." She continued to tell Mike all about her ordeal as Joe stepped into the house and took a deep breath. He was not expecting this, not in a million years.

Mike walked in behind him. "Hey, what's going on? Is that your wife?" Mike asked.

"Yes, that's my girl. I have no idea what happened. She never should have been in those woods by herself. Don't say anything to her that may freak her out. Now you see why this is far worse than death. She is still her. I can see her, touch her, smell her, but she doesn't know me." Joe looked out the window.

"Joe, she did say she feels like she knows you. Has she done that before?" Mike asked.

"No, she hasn't. The problem is how do you try to tell someone and gain their trust when they have no recollection of life with you? It's like trying to convince a stranger they need to be in your life."

"I won't even say I understand something like that. I just think you need to hold on to hope. We are stuck here for now. Have a little faith."

"Thanks, Mike. I'll try."

"No problem. That's what friends are for. I've only just met her, but I feel like I've known her my whole life."

"Anya has always made everyone feel like that. She is a kind soul." Anya walked in, opened her backpack, and emptied the contents on the kitchen table. "What is all of that, Anya?" Joe asked.

"Well, like I started to say, the last thing I remember before Dawson Forest was that I was trying to find a connection to all of this. My grandmother left me her journal, and I've found a few things that I just can't wrap my head around."

"May I look at it?" Joe asked.

"Sure, two heads—"

He interrupted, "Are better than one!"

"Yes, exactly!" They laughed, and it felt like old times.

Mike and Joe both grabbed a pile of things from the table and started to sift through all the info she had gathered. "So what happened after you went through the passage?" Joe asked.

"I walked forever. Well, it felt like forever. Then I came to a small room where I found this." She handed him the other book. "I cut my leg pretty bad while getting out of the vent into that chamber."

"Do you want me to look at it? Mike is right here."

"Sure, it still is sore. I did the best I could with the lack of supplies. I didn't have much time to throw things together." She pulled back a leg of her sweatpants, and there was the gash in her thigh.

"You actually did a great job stopping the bleeding. It looks pretty deep."

"It was deep. I cleaned it again this morning and put some liquid stitches on it. That sucked. It stung!" She laughed and wrinkled her nose. That was one his favorite things.

"Do you recall anything else about your ordeal?" Mike asked.

"I think there were about four or five men who were here in the cabin. Before they came, I was visited by three strange people. They said they bought the old Jackson farm. I didn't even know it was for sale. I also found this brochure."

Mike reached for it. "It's really faded. I can't make out many details on the cover. It is odd, to say the least," he replied.

"Can I see it?" Joe asked. "Wow, I haven't seen that in years! It's a brochure for the Georgia Guidestones, the American Stonehedge, so to speak. It is said it is the ten commandments of the occult." He turned to Anya. "Do you remember what happened the last time we were there, Palsy?" Out of habit, he brushed her curl from her eyes.

Anya stepped back and said, "I do. The men dressed in black suits were chasing us, and we ended up at Dawso—" She collapsed, and Joe caught her.

"Mike, grab those books off the couch please, and could you get some water?"

"Absolutely. Joe, has this happened before?"

"Mike, I have a lot to tell you. I wasn't sure it was all connected till right now. I'll explain after we get her settled. You're not going to believe what I'm about to tell you. In fact, if it didn't happen to us, I wouldn't believe it either. I'll tell you. It all makes perfect sense now, though!" Joe carried Anya over to the couch and lay her down while Mike grabbed a pillow for under her head and placed the water on the end table. "Anya, can you hear me? Sweetie, if you can hear me, please let me know," Joe whispered in her ear as he gently rubbed her forehead. "Come on, baby, I know you're still in there. You were starting to remember, weren't you? I miss you. Come home now. I've been waiting a long time. I need you!" A tear fell from his eye and landed on her cheek.

She opened her eyes slowly, and in an instant, he could feel the connection was back; their eyes met, and their souls were reunited. "Joe, what the hell happened? My head is pounding. Everything is rushing through my brain right now."

"Shhh, it's OK. I'm here, baby." He grabbed her and held her tightly. "I can't believe you're back! I have waited for you to come back. Jess had said it was getting worse."

"It was the headaches. They were almost unbearable, and the dreams were getting so real. They weren't dreams. They were memories. I just didn't realize it at the time. I felt like I was missing something but had no idea what. It was you! I was missing you!"

"Are you sure it wasn't your family?" Joe asked.

"No, how can I miss something I've never known? I would love to have known them, but you know we've both looked so many times, and nothing turns up."

"I'm sorry you didn't know your family. That's sad," Mike chimed in. "Did your father just leave?"

"My mother was young and got involved with a slightly older man who was married, but she did not know that at the time," Anya replied and added, "All I know is he was a security guard and moved around a lot."

"'Sounds like there is a story there," Mike said.

"I'm sure there is. Doesn't everyone have a story?" she asked.

"I want you to rest now," Joe said as he sat on the floor; he did not want to leave her side.

CHAPTER THIRTY-THREE

CHARLOTTE TOOK A deep breath as she looked in the mirror. "I can't believe this is my wedding day."

Just then, the door opened. "Look at how beautiful my baby is!"

Charlotte turned around quickly to see her mother standing in the doorway. "Wait, how did you know?"

"Sebastian had a car come and pick us up. He said he would not forgive himself if he had stolen this moment from us. He really is a good man, Charlotte. This morning, a whole medical team showed up to take over Daddy's care."

"I know he is good. There's just a part of me that feels bad about marrying him while not being in love with him. I do love him."

"Charlotte, he can provide stability for all of us and give you the life you could've never dreamed of. Stop doubting yourself. You will be happy."

"I know I will, and you and Daddy will be forever taken care of. OK, I'm ready. Let's go become a part of the Tutworth family." Charlotte gave her mother a big hug, and they walked out of the room hand in hand toward the terrace, where the ceremony was about to take place.

They were joined by Charlotte's father, who was in a wheelchair but would not let that stop him from walking his baby girl down the aisle. "You look absolutely beautiful, darling!" Her daddy leaned toward her and gave her a kiss on the cheek. "Well, sugar, I don't want to smudge all that pretty makeup off your face. I'm so proud of the woman you've become."

They could hear the harpist's music in the distance. As they walked through the doors to the patio, she couldn't help but notice there were about thirty men dressed in black sitting in a group. Who were they?

She didn't recognize any of them. *Maybe they are business acquaintances of Sebastian's.* Charlotte also noticed some of her friends and family on the other side. *How could he have pulled this off in such a hurry?* She realized just how powerful he was. There seemed to have no limitations to what he could do at any time. This was both impressive and slightly alarming. She walked down the aisle as everyone stood. The ceremony was sweet and textbook.

After they had been announced as husband and wife, they met their guests. It seemed like an ordinary wedding reception until one of the men dressed in black made a speech, talking about the infinite and prophecies, as well as a plan that was set in motion, and he did some kind of blessing. All of Charlotte's family didn't pay much attention to him. They knew the Tutworths were eccentric, to say the least. At the end of the evening, each of the men dressed in black walked up to the newlyweds and handed them each a gift in a black velvet bag. Charlotte thought it was weird but was gracious as always. This was exactly why Sebastian chose her.

After the festivities, they headed back to the hotel, and Sebastian carried her over the threshold of the doorway and placed her down. The room was beautifully covered with hundreds of flowers in every shade of purple and pink you could imagine. "Wow, Sebastian, I don't even know what to say. It's so pretty! You didn't have to."

"I know, but I wanted to. I told you I would make your every wish come true."

"Yes, you did, my husband," she replied.

"Charlotte, I have no intention of forcing you to do anything you are not ready to do. I have arranged for the suite next door as well if you'd rather sleep in there. I would understand."

"Sebastian, I married you. I am your wife. We can take it slow. I do appreciate that. It is charming, but I will stay with you here in this room. We can work toward other things in due time."

"Charlotte, it is an honor to have you by my side. And together, we will do great things that you cannot even comprehend. I will guide you through this journey under my wing. You have become a part of something so much bigger than you could ever imagine. When you are ready, we will have an heir to not only the Tutworths but also the new world we are helping shape." He gave her a hug and a kiss on the cheek. "I have a bath all set for you, if you would like, in the bathroom over there. They assured me it was fit for a queen as you are now my queen. Please enjoy and relax. I will check some e-mails and boring work stuff while you're in there."

"Thank you, Sebastian. Today has been everything I would've wanted." She hugged him back and headed to the bathroom to enjoy her relaxing bath. While in the tub and relaxing, she reflected on the day with a smile. Of course, she was a little puzzled about all of that mumbo jumbo about a new world, etc., but she knew he could be dramatic. He was probably talking about his work with the artificial rain. She settled in and started to drink her glass of champagne sitting on a silver tray next to the most beautiful chocolate strawberries—of course, only the best that money could buy.

"Hello, it's me. Yes, the wedding went well, a small investment, to say the least, money well spent. No, Charlotte has no idea. I will ease her into it. I've given her little clues, but she has no idea what she has become part of." Sebastian spoke on the phone for a few minutes.

"Sebastian?" Charlotte called out.

"I must go, Father. I will talk to you soon. I am heading back to Georgia tomorrow. When will you arrive?" he asked.

"I will not be coming. Someone needs to stay here and oversee our work. Goodbye, son. I will talk to you tomorrow."

"Yes, I will speak to you then." Sebastian hung up the phone and walked over to the bathroom door. "Yes, Charlotte, do you need something?"

"I just wanted to thank you for today. I don't know if had already."

"It is not necessary, I told you that." Sebastian almost felt guilty about convincing her to marry such a monster, but he would take great care of her and provide a life she would never have been able to do for herself. Their children would be brought up in the best schools with the best of everything at their fingertips. As for her parents, they would get the care they would never have gotten without the Tutworth money or influence. He rationalized his actions in his head. He really was torn between the man he was and the man he could be.

CHAPTER THIRTY-FOUR

B UZZ ARRIVED AT the brewery and began setting up for the meeting. *Three hours to go*, he thought. How were they going to pull this off? They had no safety net this time, no team to swoop in and rescue them if needed. It was just the ragtag group Buzz managed to put together. Most of the guys have been retired for over fifteen years from the armed services. They were all volunteering because, this time, they wanted to, not because they had to.

Buzz set up the old radio to call Joe and give him an update, as well as see what he knew. "This is Mike. What's up, Buzz?"

"Hey, Mike, how's it going there? Is Joe around? The shit hit the fan here! I don't even know where to start."

"Are you OK, Buzz? He's busy right now. Let me get him. Things have been rather odd here too."

"We are all set here. I've rounded up a few guys to go in and rescue the people in building 5 to start."

"Joe, Buzz is on the radio."

"I'm coming. Anya, just rest for a minute. I'll be right back. I have to talk to Buzz. Oh wow, I just realized you don't even know who he is."

"No, I'm coming with you," she replied. They walked out to the kitchen as he put his arm around her waist to steady her.

"Mike, put him on the speaker so we can all hear him."

"Buzz, go ahead. We are all here now," Mike said as he put the radio on the speaker.

"First of all, I lost one of my guys. It was horrible, worst thing I have ever witnessed in my life." Buzz continued. "We went down in the employee elevators, which are in the back, to avoid being spotted. We believed that it just led to the maintenance and storage rooms. When we headed down, we noticed the doors were all open, and it was not storage rooms but holding cells for people. There were bodies everywhere. The smell was overwhelming. There were men, women, and children dead and dying. It was a scene straight out of a horror film, an actual hell on earth. We also noticed many fifty-five-gallon drums with poison placards on them. I kept trying to rack my brain why they would have poison, or at least that much, at the airport. I came up blank with every scenario. I texted the pics to you, guys."

"Hold on, Buzz. I'll grab my phone and pull it up." Mike grabbed his phone. "Wow, what the hell do they need that for?" He showed the picture to Joe and Anya.

"Joe, I saw the same blue drums with that placard at Dawson Forest near the old reactor building." Anya said.

"You're right. I do remember seeing those there! Buzz, what else did you see?" Joe prompted him to finish.

"Well, we followed the hall to a large common room where there were hundreds of bodies just lying all about."

"Did they seem like they had the flu?" Anya asked.

"Hold on everyone, Buzz I would like you to meet my wife Anya." Joe interrupted.

"It is an honor to meet you Anya, I have heard a little about your story." Buzz answered.

"Joe, what happened I thought Anya was getting worse?"

"She was but," Anya interrupted "My memory came back, I just wish it was sooner or not in the middle of all this craziness." she replied.

"Timing doesn't matter, you are here now and we will finish this finally once and for all." Joe leaned over and held her hand. "Buzz, go ahead you were saying."

"Right, it was more like the bodies were just dumped there like garbage, which at the time didn't make much sense until we left the room and headed into a large concrete hall. I noticed some large sprinkler heads on the ceiling."

"What the hell would they need those for down there?" Joe asked.

"That's exactly what I was thinking. Before we could even figure it out, we were separated, and I hid near a doorway as my buddy was stuck behind a glass hatch door. Then about five hundred or so people filled the room, and all you could hear was crying. Then this man came over a loud speaker and said the most bone-chilling things about people going home and that they were worthless. He ended his rant with some bullshit about being in perfect harmony with nature. The next thing I saw was all the people grasping at their throats, and it looked like they were suffocating."

"Buzz, hold on a minute. I'm going to pull out my grandmother's journal." Anya pointed to the backpack and asked Joe to grab the journal. She thumbed through the pages, looking desperately for something. Then she asked him, "You said in perfect harmony with nature right, Buzz?"

"Yeah, some kind of BS like that. Why? Does that mean anything to any of you?" Buzz asked.

"Actually, it does, Buzz," Joe said.

Anya looked at Joe. "Do you think it is them again? Maybe they were never stopped seven years ago. I never made it to Sergeant Jackson's office."

"It sounds like it for sure. When I checked out the Pathfinder, all the information we had was gone. I figured the cops gave it to him."

"Did you never follow up with him?"

"No, he went missing, and he is presumed dead, but his body was never found." Joe continued. "After the accident, I was dealing with your recuperation, so none of it mattered anymore." He rubbed her back and kissed her on the forehead.

She grabbed his hand. "OK, so here's what, Joe. About eight or so years ago, we started receiving these weird, cryptic messages from an unknown man living in Elberton, Georgia. Oh my god, where is that brochure, Mike?" Mike passed her the brochure. "Look, there it is! The Georgia Guidestones!" She pointed to the paper.

"Hey, guys, what's going on here?" Mike asked.

"I'd like to know too!" Buzz said.

"Anya, Mike was telling me all about the Denver Airport and the hidden buildings underneath it," Joe said.

"Wait, so the airport is designed like a prison is underneath it?" Anya looked at the pictures Buzz sent them. "Do you guys see the bar codes? Every one of the bodies had a unique bar code tattoo."

"Mike, Buzz, like Anya was saying, years ago, we had started digging around about a local girl's kidnapping or murder. At the time, no one knew. She had been missing. About a year later, her body was found, and it appeared to have occult, ritualistic carvings on it. We started tracing her steps, and they led us to a place called the Georgia Guidestones. Like I was saying earlier, it is said to be the ten commandments of the occult. A so-called man named R. C. Chrtistian went into the granite company back in 1980 with a blueprint for this monument to be built. It is about twenty feet high and consists of six granite slabs and weighs over 240,000 pounds. The commandments are written in eight different languages and leave no room for interpretation. They tell the world the rules and guidelines for the new world after some type of mass extinction. He said under no circumstances could it be altered at all. Its pillars are in perfect alignment so the North Star can always shine directly in the middle of the stones."

"What do the so-called commandments say?" Buzz asked.

"Well, it says guidelines for the new age of reason, and they are outlined:

1. Maintain humanity under five hundred million in perfect balance with nature.
2. Guide reproduction wisely—improving fitness and diversity.
3. Unite humanity with a living new language.
4. Rule passion—faith—tradition—and all things with tempered reason.
5. Protect people and nations with fair laws and just courts.
6. Let all nations rule internally resolving external disputes in a world court.
7. Avoid petty laws and useless officials.
8. Balance personal rights with social duties.
9. Prize truth—beauty—love—seeking harmony with the infinite.
10. Be not a cancer on the earth—Leave room for nature—Leave room for nature."

"Wow, that literally means twelve out of thirteen people would die!" Mike said as he shook his head. "OK, and you two think this all fits together somehow, right?"

"Well, it would make sense. Mike, you told me about the murals depicting a new world order's postapocalyptic catastrophe, and Buzz is talking about thousands of people being killed at the airport." Joe continued. "I think it does go hand in hand somehow. Buzz, how are you guys going to get in without being noticed?" Joe asked.

"Leave that up to us. We've got that covered. You guys keep digging and figure out the who and the why. We will rescue some people!"

"OK, buddy. Be careful, Buzz. We are serious. These people do not mess around. If they are willing to kill off twelve out of every thirteen people, they won't go down without a fight!" Mike warned.

"All right, over and out, good buddies. We will talk again tomorrow. If you don't hear from me, say a prayer that I went quickly. I'm taking Steve with me on this one, so we are going in blind and without a safety net."

"OK, so we need to figure who and why," Anya said.

"Hey, you need to take it easy. The docs told me for years that stress and overexcitement can bring on the foggy memory and exhaustion. Please, I just got you back, baby. I don't want to lose you again. So you sit this one out, OK?" Joe said to Anya.

"Ummm, wait, are you telling me I can't be involved and that I have to just sit over here like some delicate friggin' flower while you try to figure this all out!" Anya was fuming now.

"No way, I would never tell you that. You can't because that's the surest way of making you do it! I am just asking you to please take it easy, that's all." Joe rubbed her back as he looked at her with concern.

"Well, I can take it easy when I'm dead, so let's get this done. You going to help or just stand there and watch!"

"OK, you two, even though it has been a while, it seems you have jumped right back into it." Mike laughed. "OK, all joking aside, we need to figure this out. Do we have a map of the Guidestones and the Denver International?" Mike asked.

"Sure, I can pull one up online of both. Maybe we can find some kind of clue." Anya started looking. "So we know the occult is talking about mass extinction, and the murals also allude to that as well. Hey, Mike, Joe said you showed him photos of the paintings. Can I see them please?" Anya asked.

"Yup, I have them right here." He brought his phone over, and the three of them looked at the pictures, taking it all in.

"That's horrific. How could someone call that art that is OK to hang in a public place?" she asked.

"Hey, guys, you have to look at this. It's an aerial picture of the runways at the airport." Joe pointed and traced the shape.

"Is that what I think it is? Oh no!" Anya was shocked. They all stared at the image in disbelief. The image was a swastika. "Joe, look on that bookshelf over there and grab any book that is from Germany. There's got to be something there that we have missed. Remember when we went to Helen years ago and kept noticing the sand dollar symbols?" Anya asked.

"I do. What about it?" Joe answered as he went over to the shelves and started looking through the books.

"Well, I think the sand dollars are clues my grandmother left behind so we could follow the trail to what I don't know."

"Do you think it's all connected? The Denver Airport, Guidestones, the occult and the Nazis?" Mike asked.

"The Nazis were supposedly the beginning of the new world order, right? They were trying to usher in a one-world government and mass extinction," Joe said. "Here's a book with a sand dollar on the binding!" He handed it to Mike.

Mike opened it and started looking through the pages. "Hey, guys, look here. It's a Denver address. That's actually in the downtown area," he said.

"Oh wait, I have another Denver address on this little piece of paper that fell out of my grandmother's journal. Is it the same address?" Anya asked.

"No, but it is my address!" Mike threw the paper down on the table. "Why would there be a piece of paper with my address in your grandmother's journal, Anya?"

"I have no idea. Joe, do you see anything else over there on the shelf?"

"Nah, just the one book with the sand dollar," he replied.

"Where is that book I found in the room?" Anya asked.

"Is this it?" Mike asked.

"Yup, that's it. Let's look at that one and see what clues are in there. Someone went through a lot of planning to hide that in the room," Anya said.

"Hey, Anya, can I see your grandmother's lab notes?"

"Sure, here you go."

Mike reached for the book and handed her the other one. He opened the pages and came across the formula Sonya had been working on for cloud seeding. "Hey, look at this. I knew it looked familiar. Here is Sonya's formula, and in my lab notes is the Tutworth formula. It is almost identical except the Tutworth formula has an added component. More questions, no answers!" Mike said, disgusted. "Will we ever figure this out?"

"Mike, let me see your lab notes. You told me you noticed slight changes in the texture and color while you were gone. Anything else in the entry that looks strange?" Joe asked as he walked over and looked on with Mike.

"What is this, the numbers at the bottom, 111? What does that mean?" Joe asked.

"Wait, did you say 111?" Anya walked over to look at the entry as well.

"Yes, it's right here." Joe pointed to the book.

Anya pulled out the photos of the stained-glass windows and showed and explained to them how the one in Helen had a 111 on it, and it was in the same place as the one in the cabin. "The only difference was the one here at the cabin had 333. That's how I found the journal. At 3:33 p.m., the sun shines through the window, and it casts a perfect sand dollar on the floorboards. One of the spines in the sand dollar perfectly lined up with the seam in the floor, and that's when I saw the journal!"

"So do you think the 111 is also a significant time?" Joe asked.

"Hmm, so if the 333 showed Anya something here in the cabin, then the 111 must be something to find in that location?" Mike questioned.

"But why would those numbers show up on my lab reports? My team and lab are in Denver, and you said this window is in Helen?"

"Yes, Helen. It's a small Bavarian town not far from here," Anya stated.

"'Looks like we have to head to Helen," Joe said.

"What time is it?" Anya asked.

"Ten thirty according to my watch," Mike said.

"OK, I'll grab the jeep keys, and let's head out. We need to get to this window before 1:11 p.m." Joe grabbed the keys and walked outside. As he opened the jeep door for Anya, he asked, "Are you sure you're well enough to do this?"

"Seriously, do I have a choice? It seems the world is going to hell in a handbasket as we speak, and I for one will not have a guilty conscience that I was not feeling well, so I stood by and did nothing!" she replied.

"OK then, what are we waiting for?" Joe jumped in the jeep and drove them to Helen. They would go to see Millie again and try to find the next piece of the puzzle.

CHAPTER THIRTY-FIVE

B UZZ OPENED THE door to the brewery as it was now eleven forty-five. Everyone would be there in fifteen minutes. The door flew open, and it was Steve. "Hey, you rat bastard, happy to have you on board, brother!" Buzz said as he hugged his old friend.

"Listen, Buzz, it was short notice, but I managed to get the gang on board. Smitty, Fitz, Dough Boy, Hotwire, Weasel, and Casanova are all on their way. You got us fully stocked and ready to go?"

"You bet. We have more gunpower than most Fourth of July celebrations. I'm hoping we won't need it this time."

The brewery filled up quickly with men and women willing to help. "OK, let's get down to business here. First, thank you all for coming. It is a real honor to have all of you here to help with this mission. After we discuss the specifics, if anyone is not comfortable, I will completely understand, and please feel free to go with no ill will. This could be the most dangerous thing we have done. We've had to come up with a plan in less than twelve hours and, as you know, we do not have any backup at this time.

"Our objective today is to rescue approximately one thousand people who are being held captive at the Denver International. We are unsure of government involvement yet. I have people working on that type of intel. What we do know is that people are being held in a 'quarantine' area by some kind of military branch. Whether that is a private or government group is unclear. I personally witnessed the mass murder of over five hundred innocent lives yesterday in a makeshift gas chamber that was built in the secret halls and buildings buried at the airport. I also have photos here—please pass them around—of massive quantities of some type of poison, whose purpose is still undetermined. As you can see, it is clearly enough to wipe out a few major cities. We also have information that they also have large quarantine areas in Atlanta, Boston, and Dallas. That would make four of these areas in the United States alone. We have yet to get confirmation on any overseas. However, we have heard some chatter over the airways about possible locations near Heathrow and can only assume they are set up in populated major areas with busy international airports. I'm going to turn it over to Steve for a minute."

"Hey, everyone, like Buzz, I would like to thank you as well. It takes the bravest men and women to volunteer for this. I have brought with me body cams that each of you who are going in will wear so we can keep tabs on you, as well as get live footage to help navigate the rescue and the rest of the group. We have Kevlar for anyone who will be on the front line. This will be the first of a few rescue trips to Denver International. Once we get more intel, we may be deploying a group to other areas. I and my team will be your eyes and ears down in there. Stay plugged in. Keep those earpieces in. Buzz, you wanna take over?" Steve turned to Buzz.

"Thanks, Steve. I have been down there, and nothing I say will prepare you for what you are about to experience. Stay sharp! Are there any questions?" The room was quiet. The men and women were there to do a job and wanted to get going. "All right, let's roll out."

Buzz and Steve's gang helped organize small groups, and they each took a group with them. They loaded into the military transport trucks and headed to the airport. The convoy pulled into the south side of the airport to follow the travel patterns of the other trucks. "All right, everyone, be ready! Eyes wide open and heads on a swivel."

Buzz flipped back the canvas of the truck and led them to the back door near the Dumpsters. "Here we go, team. Fitz, you take the perimeter with your team. Smitty, your team clears the way. Weasel, your team will go in first, in case you need to talk your way out of anything. Casanova, your team will be guiding the hostages out. On three. One, two, three."

The teams all had a job to do and headed in. "OK, can you hear me? This is your eyes and ears. Smitty, Buzz, Fitz, Casanova, Weasel, Hotwire, are we good?"

"Loud and clear, Dough Boy!"

"OK then, we are a go!"

"Going in hot!" Smitty replied.

"Radio silence in three. One, two, three."

Steve directed the teams. Buzz now used hand motions to push the teams forward. They were walking down the hall toward the elevators. Smitty stopped as they reached the opening near the elevator. Looking back and forth, he said, "Clear." The teams continued to the elevator, and the second group took the stairs adjacent to the elevators. Fitz's team headed down the stairwell, clearing each landing and then proceeding to the next floor. Fitz would say "clear" as they moved down each level.

Reaching the bottom, Fitz and his team headed down the hall and went into each small room, checking for survivors. "This is Dough Boy. Radio live. Status update and check in. Teams, report."

"Fitz checking in. We have no lives, all deceased in these rooms."

"Smitty here. All is clear."

"Buzz. Nothing so far. We are moving into the large dorm-type room."

"Weasel here, got nothing to report."

"OK, proceed." Dough Boy continued to monitor the screens, body cams, and audio. It was eerily quiet but not unlike yesterday. Buzz was on high alert as they cleared the dorm room.

"Buzz, this is some crazy shit," Fitz remarked.

"I'd say there are almost three times the bodies than there was yesterday," Buzz stated.

"So confirm approximately three thousand casualties?" Steve asked.

"At least maybe as many as four thousand total, sir," Smitty replied.

"Teams, be on high alert. We are approaching the gas room, where some hatches and doors automatically closed. 'Not sure if they are censored," Buzz told the teams.

"OK, put on the gas masks, Team Fitz and Team Smitty," Steve commanded. "Team Hotwire, you are standing by at the trucks? Please confirm."

"Team Hotwire here. We are standing ready. We have ten vehicles ready to go. We will get them turned over on your command."

"Good, stand by. Teams Fitz and Smitty, proceed."

"Teams Fitz and Smitty going in."

"Good god, why did someone do this!" Fitz called out.

"Stay focused, Fitz," Smitty replied.

"Come on, guys, let's get through this area as quickly as possible, please. The sign for building 5 should be straight ahead," Buzz said. "Team Casanova, stand by for retrieval."

"Teams, please be aware some of these citizens may have no idea that they are hostages and may be alarmed at the sight of us. We will have to take out the cameras to that cluster, as well as the men who will be guarding the people. How are we coming with the cameras?" Fitz asked.

"One more minute, everybody. Ready to go? Once I pull the switch, I'm sure it will alert someone that we are here," Steve said. "Go on three. One, two, three!" He gave the command.

Every team charged. Fitz's and Smitty's team headed into building 5 and were met by a group of soldiers. "Everyone, get down now!" Smitty commanded.

"Go, Casanova team!" Buzz yelled.

Casanova shouted, "Go, go, go!" His team went in and started to escort all the people from building 5 out to the trucks where Team Hotwire was; they were simultaneously starting the vehicles and helping the people into the transport trucks.

"Ladies and gentlemen, we are going to be your ride to get the hell out of here. We will be transporting you to the town of Dillion, where you will be able to eat, get cleaned up, and reach out to your family members. I know this is alarming, but I can assure you we have your safety in mind. Please take a seat so we can fit as many people in each vehicle. We will be leaving in just a few moments. You can call me Hotwire. I am a retired U.S. Army Ranger, and these are my fellow armed service veterans. Within this team of great men and women who have volunteered to come and give you a ride to safety are air force, army, marine and navy personnel."

A man turned and said, "Hoorah! I am a lieutenant in the Marine Corps." He stood and saluted the men and women who were there to help, and he also started to assist others getting on the truck.

Meanwhile, downstairs, Buzz, Smitty, and Fitz had a real fight on their hands. The gunfire was fierce. They were knocking over the bunks to provide cover. More and more soldiers were running in now from all around in every direction. "Men, we need to spread the wealth. Fitz, get over to the other side and get these explosives set up. Smitty, get the rest of the people out of here. We need to lead these assholes back into that chamber, and then we can detonate it remotely once we have the hatches locked in place and the civilians are clear!" Buzz had flashbacks of Vietnam and the gunfire he was under there. "Come on, troops, let's get it done!" Buzz shouted and motioned his hand forward to go.

There were three men waiting on the other side as Fitz walked over; a fourth man hit him with a chair from behind. He fell to his knees, and they took his gun. "What a rookie mistake, Fitz!" Smitty yelled as he and four other men started to shoot and run to his aid. "Just like target practice back home." There was widespread fighting, both with and without gunfire. The men who had been held captive joined in the fight, grabbing chairs, tables, anything they could to take down the captors.

In the commotion, Buzz noticed a man starting to retreat toward the tunnel and knew he had some answers. "In pursuit, heading toward the control room. Dough Boy, get those cameras going! We need eyes! Come on, Weasel, let's go get 'em!" Buzz called out and ran after the strange man.

"OK, we are all full except for the last transport. What's your ETA, Buzz?" Smitty called out.

"Roll out, and then we will take the last transport!" Buzz answered.

"I'll wait for the last transport!" Hotwire yelled out.

"You heard 'em, boys. Get rolling! See you back in Dillion." Cassanova said as he closed the last flap.

Buzz and Weasel entered the control room, where there was a tall man standing all alone. "There are two of us, asshole, and one of you. I'd give up now!" Buzz said to the man standing with his back toward them.

"We should just blow a hole straight through his head. He obviously knows what is going on here," Weasel said.

"Easy, man, we need to get to the bottom of this first," Buzz replied. "So are you going to tell us what the hell is going on here?"

"Do you even know who I am?" the man asked.

"Yeah, I'd say you're a worthless piece of shit. What do say, Buzz?" Weasel taunted.

"I am a direct link to the infinite, and you stupid sheep are here because we have decided till now to let you breathe our air! Worthless, you are the very essence of worthless, walking around ignorant to what's going on right under your noses. You are all sheep and finally are being slaughtered. It is time for our kind to rule. Every species has a superior version. We are that superior one. You say you want to learn, but your eyes and minds are simple and closed! The infinite is in control, not you stupid, stupid men. Do you think it's just coincidence with the violence, anger, poverty, and greed? You are doing our job for us, killing one another. Ignorant fools, could you make it any easier?"

"I've had enough of your BS. Shut up!" Buzz yelled, walked over, and placed the gun on the man's temple. "Now I'm not going to ask again. Who is in charge, and how many more are held against their will?"

"If you pull that trigger, Buzz, you'll never know the truth about your angel Faith."

"Well, ya know what, asshole? I'm done listening to you. Wait, did you say Faith?" Buzz stopped dead in his tracks. "What do you know about Faith?" He pushed the man into a chair and forced the cold steel of the gun deeper into his temple.

"Well, you see, we needed a blood sacrifice for the infinite but not just any blood sacrifice. It had to be a newborn baby boy born of a genuine spiritual, righteous soul. That would be where your Faith came in. We arranged that accident she got into, and at just the right time, we put it into play so your son—our sacrifice—would be born under the right stars above. All was in alignment the day she drove your beloved car to get it all cleaned up for you. We had been watching her for months as we have eyes everywhere, even at her doctor's office. One of us befriended her, and the plan fell into place. Thanks for helping. We were stumped about how to get her to leave her parents or her stupid church friend's side. They were always around! Such a pain, but then we arranged for you to be sent home, and it all fell into place."

"You sick bastard. Buzz, just shoot him, or better yet, just wound him and make him feel even a fraction of the pain you have felt over the years!" Weasel shouted.

"You killed my Faith and my son. You are a sick, sick man!" Buzz held back the tears, but one slid down his cheek.

"I never said I killed your son. Faith was collateral damage. Your son is alive and well. In fact, he is a very powerful man, but you would not understand any of that," Johnathon said. "The original plan had to be altered as your son was not the perfect specimen and therefore could not be a gift to the infinite. So instead, I groomed him to take over my work and the legacy that has been planned for centuries. Does that cut you deep in your soul knowing he grew up just minutes from you and I made him exactly what you dislike!"

"What do mean? Where is my son!" Buzz demanded.

"You are Sebastian's birth father. He is your son, but I made him mine. As we speak, he is setting things in motion that will start the new age of reason, and nothing you can do will stop it."

"Sebastian is my son? How could I have not felt it anytime I was near him?" Buzz was saddened at how many times he interacted with him and never knew. "Where is he now?" He cocked the gun.

"He is in Georgia, awaiting a rebirth!" Just then, he grabbed a pill from his pocket and shoved it in his mouth. "I will not allow you to have revenge. I will sacrifice myself for the infinite!" Johnathon started to foam at the mouth and convulse violently and then fell to the floor.

"Cyanide capsule," Buzz said. "We have to get out of here and get to Georgia. At least Mike, Joe, and Anya are there. I will call them and let them know. They may be able to stop whatever is about to happen till we can get there. OK, let's go. Put the last charge in that damn room!"

Buzz ran out back to building 5, where the fighting was still going on. "Hey, guys, we are hot. Let's go!" he yelled as the team ran up the stairs and out the door, locking it behind them.

Hotwire was waiting. "Get in! Let's blow this place!"

As they left that part of the airport, they saw the massive explosion as Buzz did the honors. "Hey, Hotwire, do you remember how to fly?" Buzz asked.

"You betcha. It's like riding a bike." He looked back and winked.

"All right, boys, you heard him. We are heading to Georgia."

CHAPTER THIRTY-SIX

THEY ARRIVED IN Helen, parked the jeep, and headed to Millie's. "Hello? Millie? Are you here? It's Anya. I met you the other day," Anya called out.

"I'll be right there, Anya," Milled responded. She came from the back room. "Oh hello, who are these handsome men with you?"

"Oh, I'm sorry. Where are my manners? Millie, this is my husband, Joe, and our friend, Mike."

"Hello, handsome boys!" Millie said with a smile.

"Millie, can we go up and look at that window again? I think I have figured something out, but we need to take a look once more."

"Sure, go ahead, you know where it is. Does anyone care for tea?" Millie asked.

"Thank you, but we will have to take a rain check for another day," Joe said.

"OK, where is this window?" Mike asked.

"This way." Anya led the way to the landing.

"Wow, it's beautiful. It does look very similar to your grandmother's," Joe said.

"What time is it?" Mike asked.

"It's 12:58 p.m.," Joe responded.

"So if I'm right, at 1:11 p.m., the sun should shine through the window and illuminate something, a clue of some sorts." Anya was excited.

After a few minutes, Joe called out, "Here we go. It's 1:10 p.m." The sunlight started to shine the sand dollar across the floor, but this time, it kept moving. At 1:11 p.m., it rested on a bookshelf across the room, and there it was—another book with a sand dollar on it.

"There it is!" Mike yelled out. They all ran over, and Mike grabbed the book and opened it.

"Anything?" Joe asked.

"No, not yet," he replied.

"It's got to be here. It has to!" Anya was getting frustrated.

"Wait, what is this? There is an address here in Helen on the inside back cover of the book." Mike noticed.

"That has to be it," Joe responded.

"Let's go ask Millie. I'm sure she can tell us how far it is from here." Anya started to head back out to the front room. "Millie, do you know where this address is? We found it in this book," Anya asked her.

"Give it here. Let me look at it. Well, I can once I find my glasses. Now where did I put them? Hmm, I can't seem to remember where they are. See? Don't get old. This is what you have to look forward to." Millie was walking around, looking on every table and under every chair.

"Millie, I believe your glasses are on your head." Anya reached for them and handed them to Millie.

"Ah, thank you. Oh, this address is about five blocks from here past the river and then take a right and head down there for about seven or so miles. It's an old farm, but there is a building out back that they used to grow all kinds things." Millie continued with a story about how she would visit there when she was little to feed the chickens and pigs.

"Millie, I would love to hear about that another time. How about when we come back for that tea?" Anya said as they headed toward the door.

"Bye, Millie. It was wonderful to meet you," Joe said.

Mike added, "We look forward to our next visit."

"Oh well, you two handsome boys are welcome anytime." Millie waved goodbye, sat down, and continued to talk about her time on the farm while drinking her tea.

"Anything else in that book? Or any other similarities?" Joe asked Mike.

About twenty minutes later, they arrived on the farm, jumped out of the jeep, and headed toward the building. "Hey, Joe, is that your phone ringing?" Mike asked. They all listened for a minute and stopped walking.

"Yes, it is. It's probably Buzz." He answered, "Hello? Hey, Buzz, so good to hear your voice. So what happened?"

"What happened? Holy hell, that's what happened!" Buzz continued. "There were thousands of bodies and at least another one thousand living, but we got them all out! Listen, I will fill you in on everything once I get there."

"Wait, did you say when you get here?" Joe asked.

"Yes, I'm getting on a plane now. I should be there with my team in about two, two and half hours at the latest. Where are you?"

"We are in Helen, following a lead," Joe replied.

"I need you guys to get to the Georgia Guidestones. Have you ever heard of them?" Buzz asked.

"Yes, we know all about them unfortunately. We will head there as soon as we are done here. We are about an hour and a half from there," Joe answered.

"Joe, no matter what happens, promise me you guys won't hurt Sebastian," Buzz pleaded.

"Wait, did you say Sebastian? Since when did you have a change of heart about the suit guy, and what the hell is he doing there?"

"I'll explain it all later, but I found out my son didn't die. Sebastian is my son. He's involved in some pretty messed-up stuff right now, some type of occult shit. Johnathon Tutworth was behind all of this and said he groomed Sebastian to usher in the new age of reason."

"Buzz, you have no idea what he is mixed up in. The Georgia Guidestones are the ten commandments of the New World Order. If he is there and we are right in what we are thinking, it's going to be an apocalyptic event." Joe looked over at the jeep and said, "Hey, Mike, what is that on the windshield of the vehicle? Listen, Buzz, let me go. I will see you soon, and I will try to make sure nothing happens to Sebastian."

"All right, bud, over and out," Buzz replied.

"It's a flyer, just says, 'Join us for the music festival called Illumination.' Oh wow, it's being held at the Georgia Guidestones today!" Mike read the brochure.

"OK, let's go in here quickly, check it out, and then head to Elberton," Anya said.

They pulled open the building doors and saw it was a big open space. "Nothing? That makes no sense!" Joe said.

"There's gotta be an office or something," Anya responded.

"Hey, look over there. I see an office with a light on. Joe, I'll go, you cover." Mike and Joe both pulled out the guns and started down the wall. Anya stayed behind Joe and pulled out her gun too.

"What are you doing?" Joe asked her.

"Um, did you think you boys get to have all the fun? No way!" The three of them headed toward the office. "Did you hear that?" Anya asked.

"Yes, I did," Mike replied. They got to the door and inside; everything in the office was completely thrown all over. The back door slammed just then. "Someone was just here."

"Yes, but we don't have time. We need to get in and out," Joe replied.

Anya went over to the filing cabinet and noticed there was a locked drawer; she tried to shake it open and then pulled out her gun and shot the lock right off the cabinet. "Holy shit, girl, what are you doing?" Joe asked.

"You said we didn't have time. I'm a problem solver. We had a problem, and I solved it."

"Well, damn, I guess you did!" Mike and Joe laughed. "OK, let's grab these files and head out. Mike and I will look through them on the way the Guidestones."

They gathered up the files and got back in the jeep. "Look, it's all right here," Mike said. "Sonya was working with Tutworth on cloud seeding, and he didn't like the fact she was a woman. She refused to work for the Nazis and would not give them her technology. She actually fled the country to keep it safely out of their evil hands." Mike continued to read. "They were also working on another project, but the file is missing. There's an entry that says 'area.' I can't make it out.

It looks like it has gotten some water damage on it, and the writing has bled. The file itself is empty. I think they must have changed the chemical composition of the artificial rain we were using when I had been kidnapped. That would've been the only time I wasn't around for someone to have access. I knew there was a difference as soon as I saw those notes. Remember, Joe?"

"I do. All of it makes sense, so not only were they poisoning people while we were all watching the virus world news but they also were 'quarantining' the healthy people and killing them right underneath the major airports." Joe said.

"Typical bait and switch. Look at the right hand that's doing nothing so the left can sucker punch you," Mike said.

"We are about fifteen minutes from the Guidestones. Do we even know what we are looking for? It is going to be packed," Anya said.

"We look for Sebastian," Joe said.

CHAPTER THIRTY-SEVEN

SEBASTIAN ARRIVED AT the Guidestones, and it was ready. He had set everything up and was ready to go before his wedding. He was met by his brothers. Today's ceremony would be different; it would be out of the shadows of the basement chamber at the Tutworth estate. Finally, they would have their moment in the light. Mankind would be enlightened, and they were well on their way to fulfilling the ancient prophecy and ushering in the age of reason. It was only a few moments away now; all the puzzle pieces were fitting. The brothers finished preparing for their afternoon. They were expecting thousands to come and witness their rise. The buses would be arriving any moment.

"How many souls will be here, Sebastian?" the hooded man asked.

"We are expecting about twenty thousand," he replied.

"It was the perfect cover, a music festival. It can't get any easier! Brilliant, Sebastian, just brilliant, my boy! Your father would be proud!"

"I wish he could've been here to see this," Sebastian said.

"Here come the sheep, right on schedule," the hooded man stated. Hundreds flocked to the farmland and began to party.

"Ignorance is bliss, I guess," said one of the brothers. The first band took the stage and began to play as the crowd grew from hundreds to thousands within about thirty minutes.

"Look at the excess drinking, sex, gluttony. It is disgusting. They do act like animals," the hooded man said as he turned to another brother.

"I'm sure the infinite is most proud of our actions," the brother replied.

Just then, the jeep pulled up. "Oh no, look at all the people. There has to be close to twenty thousand by now," Anya said.

"I'm going to call Buzz." Joe dialed on his phone. "Buzz, man, where are you? It's going to be like finding a needle in a haystack. There are way too many people here."

"Look, the news vehicles are here too! Great, the dawn of the age of reason is about to be plastered all over the evening news," Mike said as he shook his head.

"My team has alerted the local authorities, and they are starting to evacuate as we speak. We split up and are going through the crowd now. I see the group of men in black robes. Head west, and you'll see them. Meet us there," Buzz instructed.

"Got it, heading west now," Joe said. The crowd was so big that it was hard to make their way through it.

"Do you see them? Anything?" Anya asked.

"No, wait, yes, I see them over there." Mike pointed to the left. The three of them ran over to Buzz. As they approached him, they heard Sebastian come over the PA system, and the music stopped.

"Welcome, all of you. We invited you to all be a part of the dawn of the new age of reason!" Sebastian raised his hands high in the air, and the crowd cheered.

"They have no idea. The crowd thinks it's part of the show," Anya said.

"You have been chosen to be the gift for a higher purpose. Each one of you is about to make history for all mankind. We will be enlightened, and our new journey will begin this day. This day and each of you will go down in the history books as the day the world was reborn! We will be reborn today, with the blood from our sacrifice, offered here at the altar of the infinite." Sebastian continued.

"Go, team, now!" Buzz commanded the teams to move into place. "Joe, you three head up to the stage. Sebastian knows Mike. We may be able to get him distracted."

The crowd started to look around. "Wait, did he say blood sacrifice?" a woman turned to the group next to her and asked. Some of the crowd began to leave quickly.

TRACY ANNE BERTINI

The local authorities finally showed up and helped get people moving toward safety. "We have set up a barricade, Chief," said the deputy.

"Great, get everyone in the area behind it."

"Ma'am, you need to get behind the tape please. We are trying to keep you safe," the deputy stated.

Mike, Joe, and Anya climbed the stairs to the stage. Mike tucked his gun under his shirt. Joe and Anya had their weapons drawn. "Go ahead, Mike. We are right behind you." Joe said, and as Mike approached Sebastian, Joe and Anya both stepped out to their friend's side.

"Sebastian, it's Mike, man. Turn around." Mike kept walking toward him.

Sebastian turned around. "Mike, what are you doing? You were supposed to be at the cabin. You are not part of this. Leave now while you can!"

"I'm not leaving, Sebastian. I'm staying right here with you. We are going to leave together." Mike continued. "Listen, there is so much you don't know. I need to talk to you."

"Mike, I told you to leave!" He was getting angry.

Anya stepped closer. "Anya, stay there!" Joe demanded as they all stood there in the shadows of the granite stones; guns were drawn on Sebastian. Some of the brothers now approached and pulled weapons, pointing at Mike, Anya, and Joe.

"How could you be such a monster?" Anya yelled. "These people have nothing wrong with them. They were just living their lives as they saw fit, which is their right! Just as you had the right to live as you would like. You preach about living in perfect harmony with nature. Well, from what I see, you are creating disharmony. You took science and used it for evil. One thing we all have deep down inside is the will to do something—hell, anything. Only a monster would try to bend that will and force their twisted will on others. This is not what we are here for, Sebastian! You see miracles every day! Look around you, the sunrise and sunsets, the mountains and the oceans. How about the stars above? A newborn baby's first smile at his parents' face? The single mother who stays up to spend time with her children, even when she is mentally and physically exhausted from working hard to be both mother and father? The soldier who lays down his life for ours? The stranger at the grocery store who pays for the old woman's groceries on a whim? The rescue workers who run into danger when we all run out? Sebastian, you are the blind one. Open your eyes! How can you deny that a greater power is around us always? Even if we don't agree on what that power is, it is always here! That's the beauty of life. We all have the right to choose.

"This is not what my grandmother worked so hard for. How dare you use her work to implement your sick, twisted plan of mass extinction? The light will always trump darkness, good over evil. Even if you do not see it, there is far more good in our world than evil. Every little kindness emanates a positive ripple and causes more kindness. Johnathon Tutworth was a sick, twisted man and should never have bent your will. The fact that he stole you from the life you were supposed to have is a real crime. How can you still stand here and defend his legacy?" Anya paused. "Sebastian, he was going to sacrifice you, kill you as a young boy. Your physical limitations or imperfections were the only thing that saved you from that lunatic."

Mike added, "How can you not see it? I've worked with you now for a while. You are not this guy! I've seen you do good. Come on, just end this, put down the detonator, and we can all walk away."

"You don't understand, none of you. This world is cruel, and I am destined for greatness, and I alone was chosen to illuminate our race. This is a war for our souls. You are still so closed-minded and cannot even begin to understand. The infinite is the wisdom of the ages from every world and time. They are here living among us and have been since the dawn of our existence. We are just so self-absorbed with our meaningless gadgets and are unaware of the master plan that is unfolding right under our noses!"

Buzz and Hotwire got on the stage too and overpowered the brothers who were threatening the trio. The hooded man then rushed over. "I will not let you be talked out of this. Did you think I wouldn't have a fail-safe? That's right, you fools. He is standing on the bomb. The trigger is not in the phone, like you all would've assumed, such old technology. I needed to ensure we would have the worthy blood sacrifice to dawn the new age of reason." Sebastian was still standing on the metal plate, which apparently was on top of the bomb.

"Hotwire, any idea what we can do about the bomb?" Buzz asked.

"It must be a pressure-sensitive trigger. If he moves off that metal plate, we are all blown to hell. We need to keep even pressure on that plate," Hotwire said.

Buzz approached him. "OK, Sebastian, listen, we have to tell you something. Johnathon was not your father. He kidnapped you from your real father and, in the process, killed your mother. You are my son! I thought you had died before you were born in the auto accident with your mom, but you didn't. You had a much worse fate, a life with Johnathon Tutworth. Son, please forgive me. I had no idea. If I had known, I would have been there. He robbed both of us of the life we were meant to have." Buzz continued to walk toward him. "I know you feel like there is nowhere to go from here, but that is not true! We can build a life together. You have an amazing grandmother and grandfather, who would be so happy to know you are alive." Buzz was now standing right next to him and reached out for Sebastian's hand. "Please, son, let me take your place. Get out of here before anyone gets hurt and you can't turn back from this."

Tears started to run down Sebastian's face. "It can't be true. There's no way Father would lie all these years!" he yelled.

"He did, Sebastian. Look, it's all right here in this file," Anya said. "Tutworth stole my grandmother's lab work and used it to poison and kill millions of people. It seems they were working together on the artificial rain. My grandmother used it to help farmers. Johnathon Tutworth used it to poison the food supply, spreading that virus! That is the perfect example of science with good intention being used for evil. Sonya left clues all over so that, in the event her work fell into the wrong hands, we would be able to follow the trail. And wouldn't you know? It leads right to you and to Tutworth Enterprises." Anya was moving away from them as Joe started to push her back away from the bomb.

Suddenly, Charlotte showed up and ran up to the stage. "Sebastian, what are you doing?"

"What are you doing here? I left you at the cabin happy and visiting with your family." Sebastian turned toward Charlotte. "I love you. I had everything set up. You and your family would've been set for life. How did you know I was here?" he asked.

"I was watching the news, and they were talking about a mass evacuation, and the world news on every channel was reporting about this group of people right here and how they found out who was behind the deadly virus and the mass killings and disappearances. It appears this was going on all over the globe at most of the major airports. They reported that the death toll is at apocalyptic levels, but thanks to these people, millions of more lives were saved. The rescue efforts are going on right now live. I know this is not you! This has Johnathon Tutworth written all over it. He is the real monster!" Charlotte began to cry and walked toward him.

Sebastian started to weep just slightly. "I don't know what to believe now." He turned to look at his brothers, and they were gone.

"Sebastian, take a look at who is still here for you. Those cowards left as soon as they had the opportunity. They are not your brothers. Son, please, I beg you to let me help you!" Buzz begged Sebastian.

Hotwire said, "OK, Buzz, you're only going to get one shot at this. You need to keep even pressure on the metal plate, or that bomb will blow. You'll have to distribute your weight around his.

"OK, son, you heard him. I'm going to step in front of you with one of my feet, and then you will step off with one of yours. It's going to have to be exact."

"Sebastian, please come home with me." Charlotte began to cry. Buzz's team ushered her off the stage and behind the tape.

Joe turned to Anya. "Listen to me, I need you to go over there. You've figured this all out and have been amazing, but I will not lose you, so I can't help my friends and these innocent people still trying to escape if I have to worry about you."

"The last time we did this, I couldn't remember you. I won't leave you this time!" Anya responded.

"Anya, it is not the same. You will be safe over there, and I will join you in a minute, I promise. I need you to do this. Time is running out.

We only have five minutes before the bomb blows." He kissed her on the forehead. "I love you! Now go!" Fitz held her arm and took her to safety as she burst into tears. "Let's get this done, Buzz!"

Joe and Mike walked closer to help steady Sebastian as Smitty and Weasel held on to Buzz. "All right, son, here's to our new lives together. I love you!" Buzz looked at the men and said, "OK, last time today on three. One, two, three!" Buzz stepped on with his other foot entirely as Mike and Joe pulled Sebastian off.

"Everyone, clear the stage!" Buzz yelled. "OK, it's just me and you, Hotwire! Blue or red baby?"

"Well, isn't this cute? Me and you, last men standing, and we have, oh well, one minute and eleven seconds." Hotwire took the wire cutters in his hand and touched the blue and then the red.

"C'mon, man, stop messing around and cut the friggin' wire already!"

"All right, blue it is. Congrats on your son!" Hotwire cut the blue wire, and as the timer went off, nothing happened. They were safe!

Everyone was happy; good had triumphed over evil. The crowd erupted in cheers. The news reporters were telling the incredible story of the events of the day. "You could hear people singing 'Amazing Grace.' We were enlightened that day but not the way Tutworth and the occult wanted. Mankind is still good. You see it in your children's eyes, the sound of your favorite song, the neighbor who always has a kind word to say. Light will always end the darkness."

Joe ran over to Anya and grabbed her and kissed her. "I told you I would be right here! Here's to the rest of our lives! I love you, and I think it's time to plan that vow renewal. Happy twenty-fifth anniversary to us this year!" Joe said as he shook Mike's hand. They walked toward the jeep together, talking about the plans they would make.

Then—boom!—eleven massive explosions simultaneously went off, causing the sky to light up. There was silence and darkness all around. It looked like the world had ended. There were sirens blaring, screams from the injured, and cries for the dead.

S HE COULD HEAR the beeping of the hospital machines. "Joe, Joe, where are you!" she yelled.

"Baby, I'm right here in the bed next to you," he replied.

"Oh, I thought it was over this time. Who made it? What happened?" Anya asked.

"I don't know for sure. I know Mike did. He is in the next room. Listen, I need to tell you something. Mike and I—"

Just then, Sebastian walked into the hospital room with the physician and nurse. "Did you tell her yet?" they asked.

"No, I was just about to." Joe replied.

"Tell me what!" Anya demanded.

"Well, Anya, it seems you are once again miraculously healing yourself. We have no idea why, and I, as a physician, have only seen it one other time. In fact, you are both here today."

"What are you talking about? She turned toward Joe. "Joe, what are they talking about? Somebody, tell me something, and what the hell is he doing here!" she said as she pointed at Sebastian.

"We have found a rare . . . well, hell, a never-seen-before mutation in your DNA that allows your cells to regenerate rapidly. Almost instantly"

"What the hell are you talking about? OK, I must be dead." She closed her eyes and reopened them.

"Sweetie, they are serious. I've looked at the tests too," Joe stated.

"So your telling me I have somekind of super DNA?" Anya asked.

Just then, Mike walked through the door and said, "So, sis, our DNA is kind of cool, huh!"

"Wait, what? You're my brother?" she asked.

Sebastian walked out to the hall, crossed his hands as he walked away, and quietly said, "Excellent!"

Printed in the United States
By Bookmasters